ACCURSED

LUCIANO D'AMATO

ACCURSED

The Djinn Chronicles

LUCIANO D'AMATO

STUDIO 7

PUBLISHING

LUCIANO D'AMATO

Copyright © 2020 Luciano D'Amato

Studio 7 Publishing, a subsidiary of Studio 7 Films Ltd.

All rights reserved.

Although not a true story, this book is inspired by the real-life accounts of sleep paralysis sufferers and witnesses of the "Djinn" phenomena, including those of the author.

No part of this book may be reproduced or stored in any retrieval system, or transmitted in any form or by any means, electronic, mechanical, photocopying, recording, or otherwise, without express permission of the publisher.

www.studio7films.co.uk

ISBN: 9798644890859

Dedications

This book is dedicated to my loving family. My Mum, Dad and two beautiful sisters, my guardian angel grandmothers, and my close friend and business partner. I'd also like to thank anyone and everyone else, who has helped or supported me in any way, along the way.

Also to my spiritual guides, higher-selves, honourary ancestors, and of course the creator consciousness that is in all of us. Finally to all my soul mates, twin flames, and karmic partners. Whether blissful or painful, our interactions were invaluable life lessons in the grand scheme of things. Stay well, stay safe, stay blessed...

Dedicato al ricordo amorevole

di Nonno Piero D'Amato.

X

WRITTEN BY
LUCIANO D'AMATO

ACCURSED

LUCIANO D'AMATO

Contents

Dedications V

Foreword XII

Prologue XVI

Chapter 1 1

Chapter 2 23

Chapter 3 37

Chapter 4 64

Chapter 5 104

Chapter 6 153

Chapter 7 220

Chapter 8 262

Epilogue 273

Afterword 279

Terminology 283

References 294

ACCURSED

Foreword

Al-jinn (al-jin), from the Arabic; الجن, with the root meaning "unseen" or "hidden" and Romanized as "djinn" or Anglicized as "genie", are supernatural creatures of early Arabian and later Islamic mythology.

Djinn are believed to have been created by God, from the "smokeless fire", pre-human history. According to the earliest Islamic traditions, these creatures inhabit the same world as us, only on a different, parallel dimension.

Unlike humans however, djinn possess the inherent ability to crossover from their "plane" of existence and into ours. In some extreme cases they are even known to possess human bodies and live amongst us, disguised in plain sight.

In western theology they are what you might call

"spirits" or "demons"; the things that go bump in the night. Except they are not just "things", they are living, thinking beings and are as real as you or me…

"A'oodhu bi kalimaat-illahhil-taammahmin

sharri ma khalaqa."

(I seek refuge in the perfect words of Allah from the evil of

that which he has created.)

Sunan Ibn Majah

Vol. 4, Book 31, Hadith 3525

ACCURSED

Prologue

It's a scorching hot summer's day in 1970s Amezrou, Morocco, and the sky is a perfect pastel blue. A gentle wind carries the scent of curious culinary delights, across the small desert crossroad town in the Draa River Valley. Two young Moroccan boys are following the riverbank; skimming stones and kicking trash as they converse to one another in Arabic. The looming, dusty-red mountain of Zagora towering over them in the background.

"...countless hours had passed atop the cliff, and the poor merchant was near death." says Waleed, the taller and slightly older of the two friends.

"At the very moment when he had lost all faith, Iblis himself rose up from Jahannam and appeared to the man, offering to grant him one wish. To end his physical pain and suffering... once and for all!"

Khalid, the smaller and skinnier friend, listens on intently as they continue to follow the river.

Waleed: "Ahmed was in so much anguish, he immediately agreed to the Devil's bargain; without even considering the cost."

Noticing that Khalid is hooked onto his every word, Waleed decides to play out the pauses even further.

"But..." Waleed states, raising his index finger firmly. "Before Ahmed could change his mind, the Devil smiled and snapped his fingers - BANG!"

Khalid recoils at his friends unexpected abruptness, and trips on a fallen, rotten branch. His older mate just belly laughs and points callously, while Khalid brushes himself off. "Argh, you fool!" exclaims Khalid in frustration. Waleed continues to chuckle as he picks up his story. "Anyway... lighting came thundering down from the sky and struck the poor copper trader. He hung there from the two poles, lifeless and spread in the form of a "blood angel"."

Khalid immediately looks up to Waleed in shock. "And, what happened to him?"

Waleed stops walking and turns slowly for effect, hunching his shoulders and snarling like a beast as he does.

Waleed: "And in that split second a ball of smoldering hellfire engulfed Ahmed, transforming him into a hideous Djinn! Cursed to suffer eternity as a creature of the darkness. Never to enjoy the pleasures of human life again, but instead watch from the void as all he ever loved withered and died..."

Khalid stops abruptly and physically shivers at the thought, allowing his imagination to run absolutely wild.

Waleed looks to his frightened friend and smirks to himself in accomplishment, before proceeding along their current path.

"Hey, wait up!" yells Khalid, as he awakens from his daydream and potters after his friend.

Just as he is about to catch up, Waleed stops all of a sudden, causing Khalid to bump into him from behind. Khalid: "Hey, watch ou-."

"Shh!" retorts Waleed as he turns and motions to Khalid

to look across the riverbank. The two boys stand and stare in unison. There on the other side of the river, they notice a small group of girls giggling together as they wash clothes.

Khalid is almost immediately encapsulated by a particularly beautiful girl within the group. She has long wavy hair, which is surprisingly fair in colour, and big beautiful green eyes to compliment it. Not to mention, she is draped in the most intricate of traditional Berber garments, embroidered with a multitude of colours and patterns.

(The Berber are an indigenous, nomadic North-African peoples, famous for their colourful clothes and extravagant dress jewellery). Khalid remains transfixed for an extended moment, while his friend Waleed decides he's had enough and moves on, walking and talking to himself casually.

The girl in question finally piques her head up from her washing, just in time to catch Khalid staring from the other side of the river. The two young Moroccans lock eyes, and time seems to stand still as they recognise one other, on what can only be described as a "spiritual level".

She smiles nervously at Khalid, brushing back the hair

from her face and adjusting her headscarf slightly. Khalid smiles back, raising a hand to wave at his new amour. Yet frustratingly, the girl looks away, breaking the momentary connection with Khalid and returning to her washing as quickly as she came.

Khalid quickly withdraws his wave and pretends to be swatting flies, when Waleed sneaks up from behind and pushes him with his full force. Khalid immediately slips and falls down the rough, dry embankment and ends up tumbling into the cool, clear, water below.

Waleed and all the girls on the other side, washing their clothes, erupt into fits of laughter. Khalid belligerently stands up in the shallows and shakes himself off, red-faced with embarrassment. As he huffs and puffs, dripping wet with water, he notices a sparkling reflection shining up at him from the stream. Khalid leans in closer for a better look, ignoring the ever increasing hysterics around him.

He instinctively reaches down and pulls the object out of the silt with a clenched fist. The water, sand and clay eventually fall away, until all that is left in his palm is a ring. Although discoloured and dirty, it appears to originally be silver, with deep, symbolic engravings adorning the band and in its head a small black, misty opal.

Khalid's eyes engorge in delight; he brings it up to the sunlight and inspects it even more closely. No, this isn't just any old ring… emblazoned around the opal is a star, a six-pointed star; the seal of Solomon.

"You are not a drop in the ocean, you are the ocean in a drop."

ACCURSED

XXIII

Chapter 1

Admired

Fast forward to Bristol, England, in the early 1990s. It's 3:00am in the morning and a storm is rattling outside the windows of the local hospital. Inside one of the delivery rooms, a 33 year old British woman, of Congolese-African descent is writhing in pain. She lurches forward, teeth clenched and sweat dripping from her brow.

By her side is her Italian husband, also in his early thirties, who grips his wife's hand tightly and offers her supportive words of encouragement. As the woman gasps and pants in exhaustion, a midwife abruptly pulls back the curtains and gestures to the man to step aside quickly. The husband moves back politely, whilst another midwife enters the room and circles around the bed. The husband can only stand, back against the wall and look on nervously…

At the same time, the sounds of the woman's moans echo across the void of space, on a vibrational frequency almost completely inaudible to man. Above Earth, in the upper-outer atmosphere, an immeasurable amount of "light beings" or "souls" are dancing in harmony amongst the stars.

As the pregnant ladies groans and shrieks grow louder and longer, the mass of souls instinctively begin to separate; reminiscent of Moses and the Red Sea.

Then, from deep within the unfathomable crowd, a single spirit is illuminated brighter than the rest. The other souls look on, as this one chosen spirit is plucked from the ether and sucked down to the earthly, material plane below.

* * *

It's now noon the next day. The husband of the pregnant lady is sat with their combined family in the hospital reception room, still waiting anxiously. The husband is slumped in his chair, with his hand resting on his chin. He appears haggard and worn, with sunken eyes and a five-o'clock shadow hugging his chin. Just as he is beginning to nod off, the Doctor unexpectedly throws opens the main doors and looks to the family, smiling enthusiastically.

The family all make their way into the delivery room, where mother and child are currently resting. After they all take a moment to congratulate the wife and admire the newborn boy, the Grandfather steps forward and accepts his Grandson into his arms.

"Allora come lo chiamerai?" (So what will you call him?) he asks, while looking down at the baby and grinning from ear to ear in delight.

""Luca", it means "light"." responds the mother from her rest bed. The grandfather nods in satisfaction and continues to take in all of the boy's unique features and characteristics. He whispers to himself: "Sì…Luca. È perfetto.!"

He then proceeds to lift the boy up into the air and spin him around gently.

"Madonna mi! Lui e cosi bello, no?" (My Mother! He is

so beautiful, no?) the Grandfather says, looking around the room with glee.

They all chuckle in agreement, before the baby's Grandmother also steps forward and begins to play with the child's feet.

"Si, lui e pui bello!" (Yes, he is incredibly beautiful!) she agrees.

The baby's Father cuts in: "He takes after his Dad, eh?"

"Suo Nonno intendi?" (His Grandfather you mean?) The Grandfather quips back, throwing the Father a cheeky grin while he does.

The family all laugh out loud at this, as "Nonno" brings the baby back down and kisses him on the forehead. Finally he whispers something into the child's ear, something that although he will never remember; will come to shape the majority of his young adult life.

Nonno: "Ti benedico, mio nipote... "facia liscia"." (I bless you my Grandson... "Smooth Face").

The newborn baby musters a gurgle, looking on in confusion and wonder at his newfound surroundings. Nonno continues to pull silly faces, forcing a coo and a smile from little "Luca".

In that moment, a bond is formed between the two. A bond that goes deeper than blood, a bond formed between souls. A bond that will link them through time and space, with each one's actions inevitably affecting the other's. A bond that could turn out to be a blessing, or a curse.

TWENTY YEARS LATER...

Luca is 20 years old now, sitting apprehensively amongst a class of over fifty other students at University in London, England. He's of average height and build, with a baby face, thick brown hair and a signature silver cross that sometimes hangs from his neck.

Most of the other young-adults are sat in groups or pairs, chatting among themselves. Luca, however, sits alone and off to one side; feverishly scribbling away in his notepad. He appears to be drawing some kind of shadowy, humanoid figure, sitting at the end of a bed. In the background, behind this creature, a person sleeps on, oblivious.

The more Luca concentrates, the more intense the sketches become. With more detail, comes more clarity and after a while, the sleeping person begins to resemble Luca himself. Scattered around this key image, like a "frightening fresco", are various religious and spiritual symbols & iconography.

Just as Luca is really getting into it, he is interrupted by another student, Mohammed; who's seemingly late for class. Mohammed is slightly taller than Luca, with a slimmer frame and jet black, wispy hair. Mohammed: "Hey, can I sit here?"

Luca jumps slightly in surprise and quickly attempts to cover up his notepad, and the sketches inside it.

"Uh, yeah. Sure…" Luca replies cautiously.

As quietly as possible, Mohammed takes a seat next to Luca and starts to unpack his bag. Mohammed: "Cool drawing by the way, man."

Luca: "Huh?"

"The drawing you were doing, just now."

Luca forces a smile. "Oh right. Yeah, thanks."

Luca pulls his notepad closer (as if he has not already been busted) and goes back to taking notes.

"Sorry, I didn't mean to be nosey." Says Mohammed, as he starts to take notes of his own.

"Nah, it's cool. It was nothing really, just bored to be honest."

Mohammed looks over to all the other vacant students filling the lecture hall, and back to Luca again.

"Yeah, looks like the feeling's mutual." He whispers to Luca, whilst gesturing at the rest of the class with his thumb.

They both look at each other knowingly, before jointly chuckling under their breaths.

"So, what *were* you drawing anyway?" Mohammed asks Luca, changing the conversation again.

"Ah, I… nothing interesting."

"Really? Well you were concentrating extremely hard on "nothing interesting"."

Luca clears his throat. He wouldn't usually just share this with anyone, but Mohammed seems different; open-minded. He relents. "Well, I have these weird, recurring dreams."

Mohammed urges Luca to continue. "Oh yeah?"

"And in these dreams I'm awake, in bed but I'm paralyzed. Like I cannot move a muscle… or speak even. And then, on top of that, sometimes I could swear there's something in the room with me too."

"Yeesh, and what does it do?" Mohammed asks inquisitively.

"Sometimes it's stood in the corner of the room. Other times it's sat on the end of my bed. Once it was even stood right over me!"

"Do you know who, or what it is?"

Luca looks off into the middle distance for a moment, contemplating, then back to Mohammed again.

"I don't know. I've never seen its face or heard its voice. Yet somehow, it feels like the same person each time; almost like it's someone I know! Do you get what I mean?"

Mohammed nods. "Yes actually, I do. So what else do you "feel"?"

Luca sighs. "Hate, anger, lust, jealousy… general bad vibes."

"Well it sounds like a Djinn to me." proclaims Mohammed.

"A Djinn?" Luca repeats.

"Yeah, like a genie but usually bad."

"I've never heard of them."

Mohammed smiles reassuringly. "That's not surprising to be honest. They are not common knowledge over here. But back in my home country, they are the norm. Plenty of people have experienced them."

Luca turns in his seat, clearly enticed by the new information.

Luca: "I see. So where's home for you?"

"Uh… about 20 mins down the road." Jokes Mohammed.

Luca frowns jokingly in return. "I mean where do you hail from? What's your roots?"

Mohammed: "Tangier, Morocco."

"And what did you say your name was again?"

"I'm Mohammed, nice to meet you."

"Likewise. And I'm Luca."

The two unlikely classmates smile and shake hands, cementing their new-found friendship. Still clutching hands, Luca jumps in his seat, as if remembering something all of a sudden.

Luca: "Do you fancy coming out tonight with me and my housemates? It is fresher's week after all."

"I don't drink." Mohammed replies.

"That's cool, you don't have to."

"Still, I dunno…"

Luca relaxes his body and tries again. "Look, it's up to you. But we can just grab some food, play PlayStation, chat about films and check out the girls!"

Mohammed shakes his head disapprovingly and makes a prayer sign with his hands. "Astaghfirullah." (Forgive me God!)

"Plus, maybe you can tell me more about these djinn?" Luca adds, feigning a puppy-dog look. "Pretty please?"

* * *

Later that night Luca is sat with Mohammed near the student bar; watching on as other alumni drink, dance, sing and socialize. It's "Fresher's Week". An introductory week, where all the students are given time to settle in, have a good time and get to know each other better before the teaching term begins.

Shamus (Luca's Irish dormmate) approaches Luca and Mohammed, carrying three drinks in his hands. Arriving at the table, Shamus hands them out one at a time. Shamus: "Disaronno and Coke for "Luigi", OJ for "Moe" over here and a whisky, neat, for me…"

"Cheers." Luca says, as he accepts the glass.

"Yeah, thanks mate." Mohammed chips in.

"So, are we gonna crash this flat party or what?" exclaims Shamus, tasting his beverage.

"Sure, let's just finish these first, then we'll take a look." suggests Luca.

Shamus grins and pats Luca on the back. "Sounds like a plan Luigi."

"Guess I don't have a vote then?" Mohammed chimes in, throwing his hands up in the air jokingly.

Luca and Shamus seem to ignore their friend, knocking their glasses together and downing their drinks together in a race. Mohammed looks on as he sips his orange juice patiently, slightly bewildered by the two drinkers.

Luca, Mohammed and Shamus eventually stumble out of the student social club and make their way across the campus grounds. Various other groups of students are also dotted about; drinking, laughing, and generally having a good time.

Seemingly a little tipsy, Shamus starts teasing Mohammed about him not drinking but Luca quickly intervenes, giving Shamus an ear full. Shamus just shrugs it off and ribs Luca for being a lightweight too.

Luca pushes Shamus playfully and they proceed to pretend fight whilst laughing with one another. As the trio approach the other section of dorms, Luca breaks off the fight to go and get the door.

As he turns to grab the handle, he locks eyes with a girl. No, not just a girl.: a woman. A young woman called Arabella with the biggest ice-blue eyes, bounciest black, curly hair and the cutest petite frame. She is followed by a male, possibly a friend or maybe even a boyfriend but Luca barley notices. He is spellbound!

For an extended moment, Luca and Arabella seem to connect on a deeper level, staring passionately into one another's eyes; the windows to the soul. It's not long however, before Shamus comes barging past and practically drags Luca away from Arabella, and into the university halls. As Mohammed catches up with the other two, Luca mutters to his friends…

"She has got to be one of the most b-e-a-utiful girls I've ever seen!"

"Huh?" asks Mohammed.

"Who?" questions Shamus.

The three young men immediately turn around, almost in exact unison. Arabella is already metres away when Luca points her out to the guys.

No sooner has Luca singled her out, when Shamus instinctively jumps in front of his arm and exclaims: "Tell her!"

Luca: "What?"

Shamus: "Go on, tell her!"

Mohammed: "Excuse me, what's going on?"

Luca and Shamus continue to argue incoherently, as Mohammed takes another look at Arabella. "She looks Arabic, I can see why you like her."

Luca and Shamus stop quarrelling momentarily and look over at Mohammed.

"OK, steady on Moe. How many juices you had? Besides, I called it first." Luca argues.

Shamus interrupts again, holding up his finger. "No, not yet you haven't. Come on, tell her "Luc". Don't be a pussy!"

The boys laugh in jest at the whole situation, as Arabella continues to walk further away into the night. Luca is the first to trail off though; he just can't stop thinking about her… it's like they were meant to meet. Here, tonight. He zones out, a whirlwind of passion overcoming him, as Shamus and Mohammed continue to poke fun. Then without warning, Luca turns and runs after Arabella.

"Go on my son!" shouts Shamus.

"We believe in you!" Mohammed adds.

Luca finally catches up with Arabella and her male friend. Without hesitation, Luca gently taps her on the shoulder and smiles. She turns, anxiously.

Luca: "Excuse me, um, I just wanted to say… you're one of the most beautiful girls I have *ever* seen."

Arabella's cheeks flush a bright red and she cannot help but smile back in response. She gesticulates insecurely. "Thanks?"

With that, Luca loses his nerves, spins on the spot and jogs back to Shamus and Mohammed who are waiting back by the dorm's main entrance.

Mohammed is the first to welcome Luca back to the fold. "Nice one mate."

Shamus soon interrupts, punching Luca playfully in the

arm: "Good man! Thought you were gonna pussy out for a second there. Then it would have been a fruit-bat challenge for yah! Haha."

"What did she say?" Mohammed queries, pushing Shamus aside.

"Yeah." agrees Shamus, leaning back in.

Luca scratches his head and turns up his lips. "Thanks… she said, thanks."

Shamus laughs and pushes Luca through the entrance of the dorm building. As they make their way to the elevator, Mohammed decides to hang back for a second. He looks over to a gushing Arabella, who's now stopped in the middle of the campus with her friends, and back to Luca who is jesting with Shamus. He sighs quietly, a hint of envy in his eye before turning to catch up with his friends.

***

It's 3:30AM and Luca is fast sleep, tucked up in his dormitory bed. The room is a small but efficient space; littered with textbooks, DVDs, clothes, and other miscellaneous student items. Everything seems normal, at first. That is until a slight depression appears on the bed covers, next to Luca's feet. It gets deeper and wider as an invisible force appears to exert more pressure on the quilt.

Then there is an audible creak, as if the bed is somehow straining with extra weight. Yet nothing is visible in the room, nothing apart from Luca, still sleeping. The creaks continue, growing louder and longer with each passing second.

Luca stirs in his slumber slightly; his body seems to be trying to wake him up. As if it intuitively knows that something else is there. As if it senses that something isn't quite right.

The creases at the foot of the bed start to move, creeping their way up the sheets and closer to Luca's face. Just as this "entity" is upon him, Luca's eyes jolt wide open; fixed and frozen in fear. Luca's mind is awake but his body is still sleeping and unable to move.

As Luca strains to see through the darkness, sweat starts glistening from his pores, reflected by the moonlight through his window. Luca focuses harder, desperate to observe what is going on around him. There! At the end of the bed, hunched over like a cripple is a large, black, blurry-figure of a man. It rocks back and forth ever so slightly, a high pitched tone steadily growing louder from its direction, as it does.

Luca's eyes twitch as he tries to lock on to this thing. When suddenly it moves! Slowly at first and then with more pace, its body convulsing and contorting in curious and creepy ways. Now fully erect, it must stand well over 6 feet tall.. Finally the creature turns to face Luca. Its body twisting first, followed slowly by its head.

Sweat now pools on the crevices of Luca's face, as he looks on in helplessness. As his fear escalates, so does his adrenaline, causing his body to begin twitching sporadically. Luca pleads with himself, with this "thing", with anyone to help but it's no use.

Still it comes closer, reaching its long scrawny arm across the bed towards him. Looking around the room frantically, Luca searches for anything of use. In desperation, he notices his silver cross necklace dangling above his desk. He has an idea. Luca closes his eyes to pray.

"In the name of the Lord, leave me alone, please!"

Still it lurches forward, now inches away from Luca's face. Luca closes his eyes tighter and repeats the words.

"In the name of the Lord, leave me alone, please!"

The creature brings a big boney hand down over Luca's face, as if to smother him to death. Luca trembles in his bed at the ice-cold touch of the beast and reaffirms his prayer.

"I said: In the name of Jesus Christ almighty, go away!"

Luca opens his eyes again. And just like that, the creature is gone: vanished. Luca is now fully awake and jumps up immediately, trembling in shock and drenched in sweat. He looks around the room desperately, frantically; searching for any sign of an intruder. But no one is there. Nothing. Nada!

Clutching at his chest, Luca pants in exhaustion. Then wiping the sweat from his brow, he lets out one final huge moan and collapses back into his bed, stunned. He's never experienced a night terror this vivid and intrusive before.

Luca knows he needs to find answers and soon. Could this really be the "djinn" that Mohammed was talking about? Whatever it was, at least it's gone… for now.

"Realize that the present moment is all you have."

Chapter 2

Affected

A few days later and Luca is in the student halls corner shop, staring at his own reflection in the freezer door glass. He is assessing the undesirable effects of his inconsistent sleeping patterns on his face. The bags under his eyes hang low and his skin is a noticeably paler tone than usual.

Unimpressed, Luca throws open the freezer and grabs a bag of frozen chips from inside. As he closes it back, another student suddenly appears behind him in the reflection.

"Fuck!" Luca shouts, slapping his breast in shock.

Luca turns to greet one of his other flat mates, Tim. Tim is English, a little younger than Luca and Shamus but acts like he is the oldest of the bunch.

Tim: "Haha. You alright?

"Yeah man, not bad. Just didn't get much sleep."

"Assignments?"

"Yeah, that's it. This latest one is killing me man."

Tim shrugs: "That sucks. Gotta be done though!"

Luca looks away and sighs. "Yup…"

Tim catches on to Luca's disinterest and promptly changes the conversation. "If you're free later, come to the green and play footie with the rest of the lads?"

Luca looks back to Tim and smiles. This might be just the distraction he needs. "Sure man, I'll drop you a text!"

"Sweet! I'll see you in a bit then." nods Tim.

Luca nods back and the two men "fist bump", before Tim turns and continues with his shop.

Once Tim has turned the corner, Luca's smile fades. He

looks back to the freezer and takes one last glance at his appearance. He sighs again, deeply and walks away.

* * *

After finishing grocery shopping, Luca exits the shop and just in time to see the university bus pulling up at the stop. He grabs his bags tighter and scuttles over as fast as he can. After boarding and showing his student pass, Luca puts down his shopping in the luggage bay and heads to the back of the bus.

However as he gets to the free seats, he notices Arabella sat with her friends, giggling and joking. A sudden wave of intimidation shoots over Luca and instead of taking a back seat, he settles for one in the middle. Sitting down next to another student, who is busy reading a book, Luca nervously fiddles with his hair and clothes.

Unbeknown to Luca, Arabella has already noticed his arrival and is now turned away from her friends and watching him from behind, curiously. Still uneasy, Luca pulls out his headphones and puts them in, closing his eyes as he lets the music calm his senses.

The university bus finally pulls up outside the other

campus and the passengers promptly disembark. Luca steps off amongst the crowd, grocery shopping in hand. Momentarily adjusting himself, he prepares to push on, when all of a sudden Arabella and her friends come rushing off the bus behind him.

Luca tries to move out of their way but gets clipped in the chaos, causing him to drop his shopping bags and splitting them open on the sidewalk. The group of friends carry on laughing and joking, completely oblivious to Luca and his predicament. That is except for Arabella. She stops, turns, and leaves her friends to help him to pick up his shopping.

But Luca is already preoccupied with saving his shop and doesn't even notice it's his crush who has come to his aid.

"Thanks…" Luca offers quietly.

"No. Thank you." Arabella replies.

Luca instantly looks up; he recognizes that voice.

Beat. Luca smiles.

"What for?" asks Luca.

"You forgot already? I can't be *that* beautiful then!"

"Oh right, of course. Sorry…" Luca relents, pretending to tip his hat. "It was my pleasure, Madam."

Arabella smiles back at him and blushes: "Hehe, you're cute."

"Thanks?" Luca questions.

"Haha. Yes, that was a compliment."

"Ah, OK. I never can tell. I thought girls preferred handsome or sexy guys…"

Arabella screws up her face slightly: "Do they?"

Luca smiles back awkwardly, unable to think of a response.

Arabella: "Well luckily, you're all of those things."

Arabella hands Luca the final apple from the floor. He accepts and clears his throat: "Thanks, again."

Arabella just grins and throws Luca a cheeky, parting wink and then leaves to catch up with her friends.

* * *

Sat in his room, at his desk, Luca types furiously away at his latest assignment. When he finishes his current paragraph, he pauses and reads it back to himself, repeatedly. Once satisfied, he stretches his arms up into the air and yawns. Shaking off the tiredness, he eventually decides to call it a night, saving his work and getting up to go to the toilet.

Luca hurriedly pulls his trouser bottoms down and relieves himself into the toilet bowl. As he does, he hears a "ping" sound coming from his laptop. He glances in the direction of the sound but thinks no more of it and returns to peeing.

A moment passes and then there's another "ping". At that, Luca tries to peer his head around the door, to catch a look at who it could be. As he does though, his stream of pee wanders out of the toilet bowl and across the bathroom wall.

Luca: "Argh, shit!"

He quickly returns to his original position and finishes off, before sorting himself out and rushing back to his desk.

Practically charging into his seat, Luca wastes no time in opening up the application. A window soon pops up with a social media friend request from an "Arabella Abboud". Luca is shocked. He had an inkling she might like him back but never imagined she would make the first move!

Luca instantly accepts the request and types a message in response, simply saying "Hey!" and presses send. "Hey?" he thinks to himself, and immediately regrets it. But it's too late either way now.

Defeated, he sits back in his chair and awaits anxiously. Looking around his room, he takes a breather to let it all settle in. The girl of his dreams wants to be friends *and* it appears she likes him more than that too. "Ping"; she has replied.

Luca opens the message from Arabella. It reads: "Hey there, cutie. ;)" Reading that, Luca can no longer contain his excitement and a huge smirk forms on his face. He clicks his fingers and shakes off his hands, before diving into his response.

Afternoon soon turns to evening; evening turns to night and night tuns to early morning. The two "love birds" converse for hours, delving deep into each other's past history, right up to the present day. Luca learns that Arabella is of mixed heritage like him, but hails from Morocco.

Luca tells Arabella about his new friend Mohammed, who is also Moroccan and from Tangier. She confirms she knows of it and has even visited the place previously. They share common interests in reading, writing, culture and dancing. They've both had a similar upbringings, apart from their faiths, and both like the idea of retiring to a simple, quieter life. The two are clearly infatuated with one another and continue their flirtations long into the day.

* * *

A few nights later and Luca is again tucked up in his dormitory bedroom. This time he is led on his back; facing upwards and snoring ever so lightly. The moon throws a cold blue hue across the bed sheets and the warm orange glow of the hallway, highlights the doorframe. Apart from Luca's breathing, everything is calm and still.

That is until his eyes snap open, mid snore. (Luca's mind is awake again but his body is still sleeping, just like before). A sense of dread floods his mind, and he tries desperately to move his limbs but fails.

Paralysed again, Luca realizes it is pointless exerting himself and abandons his attempts to get up. What he can do however, is shift his perspective, even if it's only fractionally.

Breathing more intensely now, Luca musters all the energy he can and refocuses his vision around the room. That is when he first notices them…

Three shadowy, humanoid-figures stood uncomfortably still, staring out at him from within the blackness. Now visibly trembling, Luca's heartbeat goes into overdrive at the full realisation of what he has again woken up to.

Luca tries to shout, scream, call for help but no audible sounds come out of his mouth. As the nightmarish intruders watch on in intimidation, Luca's lips start quivering and the beads of sweat return to his hairline.

The more he fights and the more he resists, the more the "beings" in the room appear to grow stronger. They are "feeding" off of his fear and slowly start to step out of the shadows, one-by-one, to frighten Luca even further.

Although still not clear, Luca can just about make out that the one in the centre is the tallest of the trio. It's bigger, wider and blacker than the other two and has a grey-coloured face. The other, smaller, two which flank him are almost identical in size and shape but are completely black head-to-toe.

As they continue to approach, Luca uses his mind to try and calm himself: "It's just a dream." "This isn't reality." The creatures still come closer. "You can't hurt me; I'll wake up soon!"

The taller one; "Grey Face", stops at the end of the bed, right next to Luca's feet, which protrude rather ignorantly from under the sheets. The other two "Drones" carry on a little further and post themselves either side of Luca's bed.

Luca tries again to speak in protest, but again no audible sounds come out. He decides to use his mind again instead: "Get away from me. Don't you touch me!" He cries out telepathically.

The two Drones look to each other and then back to the Grey Face. The Grey Face calmly nods at the two Drones, who then appear to phase their hands in and out of Luca's chest, from either side of the bed.

"No, stop. Someone help me!" Luca pleads but the two monsters mercilessly ignore his cries. Grey Face just stands there too; unwavering, as it channels all its negative energy into breaking down Luca's resolve.

Seconds become minutes, and minutes feel like hours as these bedroom invaders enact a spiritual surgery on Luca's soul.

Pulling, twisting, turning and taking; the mental pain is excruciating.

Eventually Luca manages to move his eyes down a touch, giving him his best look yet at these things, up close. The only problem is his vision is still blurred and these creatures are pitch black in colour, like a living silhouette.

"Oh Jesus Christ, please give me strength. Please help me!" Luca pleads in absolute desperation.

And with those thoughts, the worker "Drones" stop what they're doing and look over to their "master". The larger one, Grey Face, becomes enraged and urges for his "minions" to continue on. Luca tenses his body and steadies his mind, repeating the thoughts again, this time with more belief and intention.

The Drones again move back and look to Grey Face in reluctance. Grey face resists for a fraction longer; lifting its boney, bent fingers in Luca's direction and pointing menacingly. Luca repeats his command one more time, louder and more intense: "IN THE NAME OF CHRIST, I SAID LEAVE!"

And just like that, the two Drones drop back into the shadows, disappearing back to whence they came. But Grey Face refuses, instead glaring furiously at Luca for an extended moment. Its whole body vibrates rapidly in anger (or discomfort) as it retreats its skeletal looking hand back. Then to it dissipates into the ether like it was never even there.

And just like that -WOOSH! The negative energy is literally sucked out of the room, almost instantaneously and Luca is able to jump up out of bed. He falls over onto the floor, coughing and spluttering. Grasping at the carpet, he crawls across the bedroom with what little energy he can muster.

Arriving at the doorframe, Luca reaches up and flicks on the light switch. Slamming his back against the door and sliding down onto his bum, he scans the room intently.

Yet again though, no-one (or no-thing) is there. Settling on his laptop screen, Luca notices that the time is 2:33AM. He also sees that he has an unread message from Arabella.

"The only temple that matters can be found within yourself."

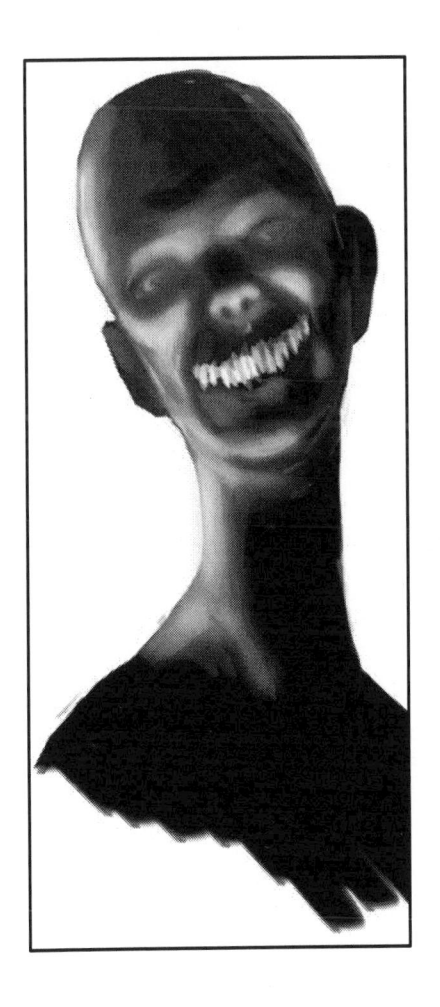

Chapter 3

Afflicted

A few weeks have passed since Luca's last, late-night visit. Thanfully the weather is warmer today and he and his friends are out at the local park, enjoying the sun. Tim, Shamus, and some other boys from their year are playing football over on the main field, while Luca is led on the grass with his head on Arabella's lap.

She is playing with Luca's long curly hair, while he picks at daisies in the grass. As he looks up at the sky, on this especially clear day, Luca sees what appears to be a grid encompassing the earth.

The grid is semi-transparent and grey in colour, blanketing everything above him and patterned like a cross hatch weave. Luca continues to marvel at this oddity and is about to inform Arabella, when one of the guys playing football shouts aloud: "Heads up!"

This causes Luca to look over to his friends, just as the football drops into view, about 20 feet away, and bounces off to one side.

Looking back up to the view above, Luca is startled when the grid is no longer visible. He squints in frustration, and adjust his positioning but still nothing becomes apparent. Was it real? What did it mean if it was? And more importantly, was this somehow connected to the djinn?

"Arabella…" Luca says, looking up lovingly.

"Yes Luc?" she responds playfully.

"Have you ever heard of sleep paralysis?"

"Um… what's that?"

"Like, have you ever woken up in the night but not been able to move?"

Arabella stares into the distance, thinking back.

"No, not that I can remember."

"Oh, OK." accepts Luca sheepishly.

"Why do you ask babe?"

"Ah, nothing…"

Arabella pleads: "No, tell me."

Luca looks uncomfortable. "It's not important. Don't worry."

Arabella immediately stops playing with Luca's hair and leans over to meet his gaze, gracing him with a growl and a glare. Luca relents and sits up properly to face Arabella.

"Right, so I keep having these dreams, where I wake up and I'm still in bed. Like, exactly how I went to sleep but now I'm paralysed and I can't move!"

Arabella continues to play with Luca's hair: "That is weird…"

Luca elaborates: "There's more. Sometimes, when I wake up, there's other people in the room with me."

"People like who?" exclaims Arabella.

"I don't know. I can't see their faces." replies Luca.

"Hmm."

"What I do know for certain is, they want to hurt me."

"How do you know that?"

"I can feel it. Like *really* feel it." Luca explains. "It's like the room is filled with negative energy. It's so thick and draining, you can hardly breathe."

"OK, this is creeping me out now." Arabella admits, throwing up her hands.

"Right! Well imagine how I feel." suggests Luca, running his hands through his hair.

Arabella waves her hands apologetically.

"So, what happens then?" she asks.

"Well, not much yet. They just seem to want to scare me."

"Ugh. Sounds like my worst nightmare."

"The only way it seems to stop, is if I pray or call out some holy name."

"Now that is interesting... maybe it's just stress from all this uni stuff?" offers Arabella.

Luca looks off to his flat mates playing football and thinks about Arabella's comment.

"Yeah, could be." he says finally, looking back up to Arabella.

"Probably doesn't help being bipolar... or having recovered from brain surgery either."

Luca instinctively withdraws and throws the handful of daises he collected into the wind.

Arabella realises this and strokes Luca's face affectionately for support.

"A family friend of mine knows this person who does "Reiki". It's a spiritual way of cleansing the body of negative energy. Maybe we should try it?"

Luca holds Arabella's hand as it rests on his face.

"It's worth a shot. I'd try anything right now."

"Good. I'll ask him about it." Confirms Arabella cheerfully.

"Oh, there's one more thing…" adds Luca.

"Yeah babe?"

"What do you know about djinn?"

Arabella pulls back her hand, the smile quickly fading from her face. Luca notices this sudden change in her demeanour and sits up attentively in response; she does know something.

* * *

Arabella and Luca return from the park and back to Arabella's dorm room. Once inside Luca takes a seat on the bed, while Arabella starts rummaging around in her draws. After a quick search, she pulls out a jar with various trinkets and jewellery inside.

Pouring the contents on the table, she singles out one worn down ring in particular. The ring has a distinctive emblem etched onto its face. Not just any old emblem either. It's the Seal of Solomon aka: the six pointed star or hexagram.

Arabella rolls the ring around between her fingers and then passes it onto Luca.

Arabella: "My Dad gave it to me when I was younger, not long after he split up with my Mum."

"Who's is it?" Luca inquires, inspecting the ring himself.

"It's King Solomon's ring, apparently…" answers Arabella. "Or one just like it, anyway."

Luca moves it around in his palm, examining it more closely. It does look old but there is no way to tell if it is authentic or not.

Arabella continues: "The story goes that God was so pleased with Solomon's service as King, that he decided to gift him with a wish. A wish for anything he wanted."

Luca offers the ring back to Arabella, satisfied.

"Solomon surprised God by only asking for one simple thing: wisdom. For the sole reason that he could continue to rule his Kingdom well and in God's honour."

Arabella accepts the ring back from Luca, takes another last look herself and then returns it to the jar.

"God was so pleased with this answer because it wasn't selfish or wasteful. So he imbued Solomon with a magic ring as a gift. This ring was not precious because of its carats, however.

It was special because it had the power to control demons or spirits; what we know in Islam as the Djinn."

Arabella finishes returning all the items to the jar and then places it back in her draw. She continues: "Allora (well then), no one knows what happened to the ring; or rings, after the King died. But… my Dad found this in a river in Morocco when he was young. He's kept hold of it ever since. Before passing it on to me, that is."

"Wow! This is so cool. It can't just be coincidence, right?"

"Well, that's what he told me anyway. He also said the black opal comes from Lucifer's crown, which broke off when he first fell to Earth." shrugs Arabella. "So who knows? I didn't say it was *definitely* real. Besides, he wasn't the most trust worthy person himself…"

Luca shudders at the thought of it all.

Luca: "Still, it's creepy right?"

Arabella: "I guess. If you believe in that sort of stuff?"

"Well, do you?"

"Luca, I'm Muslim. It is part of my religion to believe,

so I kind of have to. BUT I generally try not to give it much thought. The more you do, the more you can attract them." Arabella explains in an animated fashion.

"The more you attract what?" Luca quips, cheekily.

Arabella stops playing with her knick-knacks and throws Luca a salty look. Luca just giggles goofily in response.

"I'm just playing. Look, let's forget it now anyway. Fancy some food?"

Arabella relents and jumps on Luca's lap, wrapping her thighs around his waist and throwing her arms around his shoulders.

"You *do* know the way to my heart. Haha!" she says.

Luca winks and puckers up his lips. Arabella slaps his mouth playfully and pretends to pull away but Luca pulls her close and looks seriously into her eyes.

Arabella stares back intensely and there's a moment's pause, as the tension steadily rises in the room. Then almost symbiotically, they embrace each other tightly and kiss passionately for the first time.

* * *

Luca and Mohammed are sat next to each other in an early morning lecture. Most of the other students are either watching the picture being screened, playing with their phones, or whispering among themselves.

Mohammed is dutifully taking notes on the film, while Luca is pretending to as well but actually reading a book on symbology entitled: *"The Symbol Detective by Tony Allan"*.

The current page which Luca is reading covers the topic of King Solomon and his related sigils, with an illustration at the bottom which bears an uncanny resemblance to Arabella's Dad's ring. Mohammed glances over momentarily from his writing and notices what Luca is reading.

Mohammed: "Still having those dreams huh?"

Luca flinches at being disturbed but is thankfully snapped from out of his daydream.

Luca: "Uh, nah. Not for a while now actually."

"What's that for then?" Mohammed asks, gesturing to the book on symbols that Luca is holding.

"Ah, just a bit of research. Can't hurt right?" says Luca, closing the book promptly.

"I'd let it go if I was you…" Mohammed puts down his pen and turns to Luca. "Real or not, driving yourself mad looking into it, certainly isn't going to help."

Luca scoffs at Mohammed's remark and then quips back, deflecting: "Yeah, you're probably right. Unfortunately, I'm a stubborn Bastard!"

They both chuckle at the comment, disturbing the previously distracted lecturer; who swiftly shushes the classroom. Luca and Mohammed drop their heads and carry on their conversation regardless.

"How's you and Arabella going anyhow?"

"Yeah, we're good at the moment."

"You two… you know?"

Luca kisses his teeth and looks away.

"You *know* we haven't. She's Muslim, like you."

Mohammed nods his head agreeingly.

"Just checking. You never know these days."

"Nah, she's not the type. So don't worry. Haha."

"I'm sure but how's that working out for you?" questions Mohammed.

Luca sucks in through his teeth.

"It's a struggle, I'm not gonna lie." he admits. "But it's her life, her choice, right?"

"Exactly. Just keep strong, it'll be worth it in the end."

Mohammed picks up his pen again and pretends to take more notes in an effort to divert the lecturer, who is piquing his head again.

Luca waits for the lecturer to become distracted again, and then slyly slides closer to Mohammed, whispering more appropriately.

"Yeah, and when's that then?" Luca asks Mohammed, half joking.

"Well, when you get married." states Mohammed as matter-of-fact.

"Haha. Fair, but when's that?" Luca adds cheekily.

"Hm. Probably when she introduces you to her Dad."

"Well that's not likely to happen anytime soon. They don't get on apparently."

Mohammed winces.

"Oof, might be waiting a while then." Mohammed teases.

Luca suddenly looks sullen; a sign of his true feelings on the whole situation. Mohammed catches a glimpse of this and offers another joke to break the tension.

"Oh well. If it doesn't work out, you'll still have porn!" Luca forces a laugh but it's clearly half-hearted. He picks his pen back up and is soon looking off out the classroom window. Not wanting to cause further offence, Mohammed decides to stop prodding and diverts his attention back to the lesson.

As the lecture continues on, Luca grips his pen tight. He wonders why he feels emotionally confused when instead he should feel happy. He grasps the pen tighter and bites his lip harder until -CRACK, the pen snaps in two.

Luca winces and drops the broken parts onto his notepad. He watches on apathetically, as the jet-black ink pools in the centre of his palm. The ghastly image of a ghoul seeming to eerily take shape momentarily, before bleeding away…

* * *

Tim, Shamus, Luca, and a handful of other students are huddled outside a local bus stop. Half cut, they are all jesting with each other and having the "craic". They are all smartly dressed, either in shirts and slacks or smart jeans and shoes. It's another student night at one of the area's best clubs.

Without warning, the gaggle of guys go quiet for an extended moment. There's a cough and splutter from the crowd in the cold night air. Someone even audibly shivers, until Tim breaks the ice.

"Right then lads. Best heavy weight boxer of all time. Go!"

Shamus takes a swig of his bottle of Corona and tuts. "Ali, of course."

Tim rolls his eyes, unimpressed. "Agh... obvious answer! Questions too simple. OK, OK, best *modern* heavyweight boxer."

"Klitschko then!" Shamus shouts, throwing his hands (and half the contents of beer) up in the air.

The gang all move away from the immediate vicinity, as the cold beer slaps the crisp concrete.

"Ugh. Watch it "Shame"." begs one of the other guys, wiping the wet off his shirt.

Luca briefly looks up from his phone and chucks his two cents in. "We all forgotten about Tyson already?"

Tim and Shamus immediately look at one another and then back at Luca. Together: "Here we go…"

"What?" says Luca, turning up his lips and gesturing with his hands.

"Just 'cos your long-lost uncle or whatever trained him. What is he to you again, anyhow?" replies Shamus.

Luca grins. "Unconfirmed to be honest. Probably bullshit. But we do have the same surname."

Tim pulls out a cigarette and lights it. "Good old Gus."

"It's Cus, actually." Luca corrects.

"Whatever." shrugs Tim rudely.

"You asked, dick." mutters Luca as he continues to play with his phone.

"You're all forgetting the real MVP though guys." interrupts Shamus.

"Oh yeah, who's that?" Luca contemplates, mockingly.

Shamus downs the rest of the beer and throws the bottle over his shoulder.

"Me, of course!" he shouts, flexing his arms.

"Ugh." scoffs Tim.

"Did you really have to litter?" Luca sighs.

Shamus turns around and starts to sing and dance on the spot. A very flaky rendition of *"Wonderwall by Oasis"* was on the cards that night.

Tim finishes the final drags of his cigarette and flicks it down a drain on the side of the road.

Tim: "Whatever weirdos. And heads up, the bus is here."

The guys all finish off their drinks and promptly tidy up their image, just in time for the double decker bus to pull up at their stop.

"And you, get off your phone. It's lad's night!" demands Tim.

Luca chomps down on the gum in his mouth louder and sticks up a middle finger without looking: "Dicks." he whispers. The guys all proceed to rush on, whilst Luca waits behind an extra few seconds, in order to finish his message.

It reads: "Hey, hope you're OK. Been trying to get hold of you. Let me know where you are."

He checks over it hastily; presses send and then joins the rest of the lads, just in time.

* * *

Fast forward to later that night, Luca and his friends are onto their third club and lord knows what number of drinks. The later the night goes on, the less appealing the type of clubs still open. This just happens to be one of those clubs.

A real dive, full of drunks, undesirables and the people who just will not call it a night. The music is thumping, the lights are low and there is the unmistakable smell of sin in the air.

Luca and Shamus are dancing away on the main dance floor. Around them are other scattered groups of revelers. Everyone is either drunk, high, or looking after someone else at this point and it shows.

The boys probably would have left by now, if it were not for Tim getting off with a random girl he pulled, over in the corner of the room. The lively RnB song that is playing is coming to its end and the DJ is lining up the next track. As the music breaks, Shamus leans over to Luca and shouts in his ear. "I'm getting another drink. Want one?"

Luca continues to bop his head as he struggles to hear. Tim glances over at the boys but before he can do anything, the unknown girl has already started to suck his face again.

Shamus repeats the question while motioning "drink" with his hand. Luca nods and leans forward, shouting. "Water please."

Shamus nods in acknowledgement and attempts to "moonwalk" off the dancefloor, bumping into a pair of girls on the way. Probably intentional, although Luca is too drunk to know for sure.

Luca laughs to himself and continues to dance, letting the music take over his body. He opens and closes his eyes repeatedly, partly because the alcohol is affecting his vision and partly because it feels so good with the music.

As the new beat picks up pace, so does Luca's dancing. Although he is not the most overtly confident person, when it comes to dancing; nothing can get in his way.

While he repeats this pattern a few times, he notices a

girl staring at him seductively from across the dance floor. She seems to be alone but Luca cannot be certain. He tries to ignore her looks but there is something about her, something that gets under his skin. Like an itch he couldn't help but scratch.

That's when she locks onto Luca and smiles provocatively over at him. He smiles back and uses the music to run through his body. He closes his eyes again and feels the beat once more, letting it guide him.

He turns and spins, drawing the attention of those who were sober enough to notice; he is really shining. Luca opens his eyes at last and there she is, making her away across the dancefloor. As she gets closer, she slowly turns around, purposely showing off her ample figure.

Luca instinctively looks away and uses it as an excuse to find Shamus, however he is nowhere to be seen; not even at the bar.

Before he knows it, Luca's eyes are back on the girl. She is now dancing sensually in front of Luca, occasionally brushing her body against his. Luca decides against his better judgement to dance with her but attempts to keep some semblance of distance. Every so often he attempts to look around for Shamus again.

What feels like minutes pass, until eventually he spots him, talking to yet another girl by the toilets. Shamus has his shirt top unbuttoned and she is feeling his chest hairs. Luca cringes slightly and turns back to his unwanted, impromptu dance partner.

She's now writhing up and down on the spot, allowing Luca an unfiltered perspective of her cleavage. He smiles awkwardly at the girl and turns around again, half-heartedly one-two stepping to the beat.

Somehow the girl is still unperturbed and instead edges in closer, rubbing her hips against his as if this were some sort of mating ritual…

"Hi." the girl says loudly, amongst the thumping music bellowing from the speakers. Luca turns and nods back politely.

"My name's Mischa." she continues.

Luca relents: "Hey, I'm Luca."

Mischa: "Want to dance?"

"Uh..." Luca looks around for an excuse to leave but it is too late. Shamus is now gone from sight and Tim is right this moment heading to the smoking area, arms wrapped around the girl he was kissing earlier. Luca sighs.

He turns back to the girl, who unbeknownst to Luca, is sneakily snaking her arms on his shoulders. Luca is uncomfortable. He takes her hands away and carries on dancing. She turns around again and presses herself against Luca, grinding up and down sexually.

Luca holds his hands up in the air and looks around guiltily but no one is paying attention anymore. Plus, Shamus and Tim are still A.W.O.L. with their new prospective partners.

Mischa stops grinding and turns back around, throwing her arms back around Luca's neck and leaning in for a kiss.

Luca turns his face away.

Mischa, offended: "What's wrong, you don't like what you see?"

Luca: "It's not that."

"What then?" she asks? "Don't you wanna fuck me?"

Luca laughs it off playfully, scanning the room desperately as he does. Mischa grabs his cheek and pulls him in close.

"I *want* you."

"Thanks. But I'm taken."

Mischa appears to get serious, fast. She stops moving and stares directly into Luca's eyes. "I said, let's fuck."

Luca meets her gaze. She grabs his hands and puts them on her chest. She looks deeply into his eyes; they appear dark and hypnotic with a hint of crimson red alluding to something darker lurking behind. She laughs devilishly and winks.

The visceral lights, sounds and smells of the club all combine to create a cacophony of sensual overload that causes Luca to "black-out".

His lack of willpower has forced his body and spirit to become detached, transforming him into what is essentially an empty vessel. A prey for any malevolent entity, that may wish to exert any and all forms of mischief and mayhem.

* * *

Early that next morning and Luca is fast asleep, back in his dormitory bedroom. However he is not alone. The girl from the club, Mischa, sleeps peacefully next to him. Littering the room around them are clothes strewn across the desk and empty bottles on the floor.

Whilst Mischa seems to sleep on blissfully, Luca's movements tell an entirely different story. He is twitching, turning; restless. He seems to be having another night-terror.

As Mischa pulls the sheets tighter and snuggles into her pillow, Luca's eyes shoot open wide; a terrified look on his face.

He lays there, wide-eyed and shocked as a tall, dark, scrawny figure slips out from the shadows of the clothes rails. Lucas eye's flicker open and closed in rapid succession, while the creature's oily-black form slides across the room like darkness incarnate.

The closer it gets, the more Luca shakes. Luca tries to keep his eyes focused on it but the monster moves unlike anything of this Earth and seems to defy all known laws of physics.

Suddenly the anthropomorphic "mist-man" is upon Luca

and bearing down on him as he sleeps. Luca's vision is blurry but it does not matter, he can practically feel the grotesque, putrid, rotting features of what stands before him.

Luca starts to toss and turn violently, the creature clawing its way closer across Luca's bed. It reaches out its hand, just like all the visitors before it; extending its elongated arms in inhuman ways until it is inches from Luca's still paralysed face.

Luca musters all the energy he can and screams with his mind: "NOOOOOO!"

Awaking from what must have been a dream within a dream, Luca looks around the room, dazed and confused. He follows his arm and to his shock, realises his hand is open around Mischa's neck.

Breathing heavily, Luca instantly withdraws his arm and hides it behind his back. He shakes his head in disbelief and slips back quietly into his previous sleeping position.

Luca looks up to the ceiling with a distinct look of horror on his face. He sluggishly wipes the sleep from the cracks of his eyes and contemplates the situation he's gotten himself into. He was lucky he didn't wake the girl, imagine her finding him with his hand on her throat!

Moreover he's just made the biggest mistake and cheated on the girl of his dreams. What has he done? Luca sighs and checks the time on his wristwatch, which is still wrapped around his wrist. The time reads 3:03AM. (The beginning of what is also known as the "Witching Hour" or "Devil's Hour").

"Knowledge comes from learning. Wisdom comes from living."

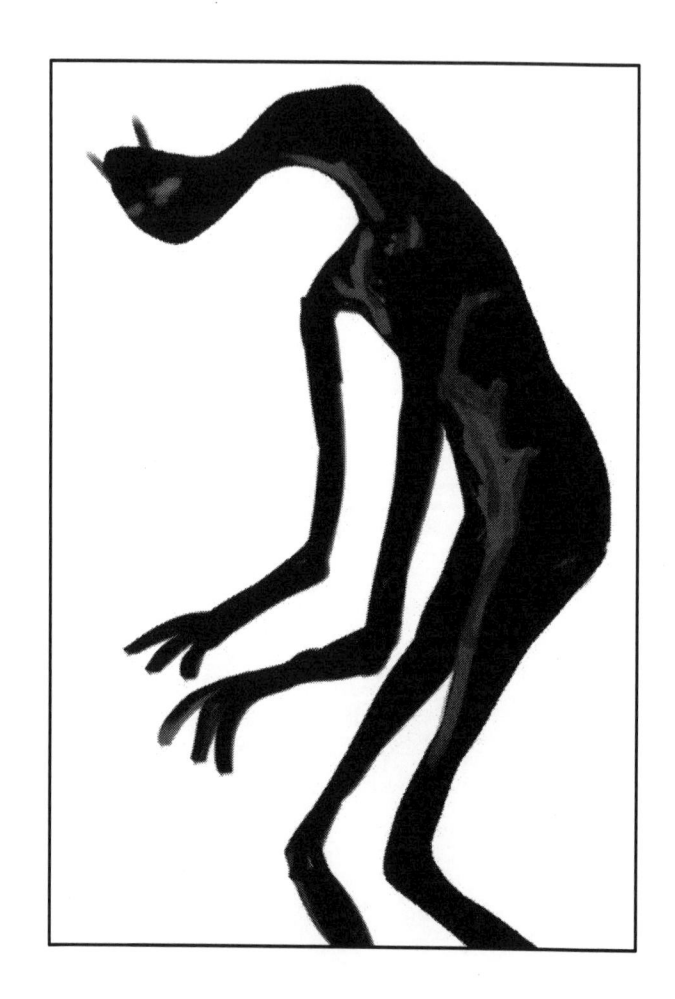

ACCURSED

Chapter 4

Arrested

A few days have passed since Luca's fatal mistake. He's now back at university, sat in on a lecture about the *"Epic of Gilgamesh"*. This is a subject which would usually fascinate him but things have not been the same since that night out. He is rattled, cagey and sporting the sunken features of a zombie.

Around him, his fellow classmates listen on intently and take notes acutely with their laptops and notepads. Luca however just sits there, staring blankly off into the middle distance. Once again he is away with his thoughts, overthinking and tormenting himself for missdoings. As the lecture carries on, Luca is gradually enticed into a dangerous type of daydream.

Whilst he struggles to stay awake, the lecture room around him wobbles and warps, like a hallucination or psychedelic trip. The colours and shapes all morph and meld in obscene ways, the blacks in particular stand out as alive and sentient.

Luca is mesmerized, no dumbfounded. The colours have seemingly put him under some sort of the spell. Then the colours suddenly start moving in a more focused and structured way, until they form a completely new setting around Luca.

Luca is now stood in a field. On the other side is Arabella, swaying with the wind in a beautifully simple, plain white dress. The field looks like one they went to on their very first dates but he cannot be certain. It is twilight, the sun has almost set and the moon is big and bold the sky, giving the effect of an enormous nightlight.

Luca opens his mouth and calls Arabella's name but no words come out. He tries again, this time reaching out with his hands. Still, no use. He goes to call a third time but before he opens his mouth, Arabella stops swaying. She slowly turns around and as Luca goes to run to her, she reveals her face to be that of Mischa's instead!

Luca's excitement dissipates almost instantly. His arms fall back to his sides. He closes his eyes and opens them again. Boom; Mischa is inexplicably stood right in front of him. Luca jumps back, startled and almost falls flat on his back.

Mischa leaps forward again, attempting to embrace Luca but he refuses and steps further away still. Mischa stops and laughs devilishly, her appearance morphing and moulding into that of a ghoul or spectre. "Aaaagggghhhh!" she screams as she rushes towards Luca.

Before she can get hold of him however, Luca snaps back to reality and is awake in the lecture hall once more.

He is visually shook, confused, and drained. It seems like whatever that experience was, sucked a lot of energy out of him. Taking a moment to centre himself, Luca soon seems to calm down. Sitting solemnly in his lecture seat, Luca tries to process the information overload. At the same time, the other students are already starting to pack up and leave.

A bewildered Luca shakes off the paranoia and then goes to leave himself, when out of the blue, a mysterious hand reaches out and touches him on the shoulder. Luca jumps instinctively, dropping his textbook.

"Woah, you OK mate?" apologises Mohammed.

Luca breathes a sigh of relief and picks his book up from the floor.

"Shit, sorry mate. I was miles away there!" he responds apologetically.

"Come on, let's get out of here." Mohammed says forgivingly, pointing at the cleaning ladies entering the classroom from the back. "Unless you planned on giving them lot a hand?"

Luca scoffs and looks around the half-empty room. He shakes off any remaining bad vibes, grabs the rest of his things and makes off with Mohammed.

Luca and Mohammed are walking towards the university bus stop together. They are chatting about the lecture and their thoughts on the ancient adventure of Enkidu and Gilgamesh. After they exhaust that topic, Mohammed begins to pry about Luca and Arabella's relationship.

Luca is overcome with guilt and instead deflects the questions, in favour of generic small talk. As they approach the shelter, Mohammed starts to peel off in another direction, towards the local town centre.

"Alright then buddy, I guess I'll see you tomorrow." Mohammed says.

"Cool, yeah, see you then!" Luca replies.

Mohammed: "You sure you're OK though?"

Luca: "Yeah, I'll be fine. Just need a proper night's sleep, that's all!"

"Good idea. Call me in the morning then."

Luca does not respond right way; something is on his mind again. Mohammed reaches out a hand and waves it front of Luca's face sarcastically.

"Hello? Earth to Luc!"

Luca slaps his head in stupidity. "Uh, yeah, sound. Chat in the morning…"

With that, Mohammed nods, chuckles, and walks away. Meanwhile, a nervous Luca attempts to find a place in the growing que. Suddenly his phone beeps and vibrates from within his trouser pocket. He pulls it out and opens the message, it's from Arabella. It reads: "Hey baby, I'm back! XXX"

Luca looks worried at the news, instead of excited like he should be. He closes the message and returns the phone to his pocket, before getting on the bus along with the horde of other students.

* * *

Later that same night, Luca is sat alone at his desk; laptop open. After mumbling words of encouragement to himself, he switches the computer on and types the word 'Djinn' into the search engine. A list of relevant links soon populate the window and Luca beings scrolling through the options.

He decides to start at the beginning and follows a link to a site that explains the history of the djinn mythology. It all starts with their creation by God, or Allah, during the Genesis story but before Adam and humanity.

They were the second creation (after angels) to inherit

some sort of sentient consciousness but they also had the gift of "free-will" as humans would come to do. The only difference being that the djinn cannot create or manifest in the physical reality, the reality that also seems to be the most sought after.

The first of God's creations; the angels, were beings made of pure light. However, their role as "architects" required their place to remain in the "heavens", beside God's throne.

The djinn on the other hand, were a mysterious race of ethereal beings, apparently birthed from the smokeless blue fire (electricity or plasma energy) and given free reign of a young Earth.

The depictions of these ancient creatures vary slightly between different religions and cultures. One overarching theme though, is their pitch-black pigmentation, crimson red or yellow eyes, and the apparent ability to shapeshift their form at will.

Over time though, something changed in the creator's heart and he was no longer satisfied with his second creation. As such, he decided to create a third and final class of sentient, anthropomorphic beings; humans.

Humans were made from "clay" or the "salt" of the

earth, so when the creator decided to release his new children into the world, he did it on the material plane rather than the ethereal. This is why the djinn cannot be easily seen by humans, they are in fact living in a parallel dimension to earth.

Anyhow, the story goes that the most revered of the djinn race was "Iblis" (he who despairs), also known as "Azazil" (scapegoat). He was so intelligent, beautiful, and talented, that he was allowed to sit among God and his angels and even contributed to his counsel.

Unbeknown to the rest of the Elohim (Archangels) however, Iblis had hate in his heart; a hate that would change the destiny of creation forever. You see, for all Iblis' talents, he was also just as prideful.

So egotistical in fact, that when God introduced humans to his council (Adam & Eve), Iblis refused to bow down to them. He argued that angels and djinn were made of light and fire and possess extraordinary abilities that humans could only ever dream of.

Iblis' anger was so insipid, that God (Allah, the creator) was forced to banish Iblis from his throne, his council, and all the heavenly realms. Iblis was also stripped of his title, given the new name "Shaytan" (the accuser/adversary) instead and then forcibly exiled to the astral plane below, along with the rest of the djinni.

Yet Shaytan did not stop there. Instead he rallied the djinn race behind him and polluted their minds about how the "unrighteous" humans had upended their rule unjustly, taking what was rightfully theirs. To this day, Shaytan rules over the ethereal realms of Earth and even has a stronghold over the material plane as well.

He does this with the help of his "Ifrit", particularly evil and manipulative djinn who are loyal to Shaytan alone (in Christianity they are referred to as the "Watchers" or the "Nephilim").

These Ifrit, along with other djinn loyal to Shaytan, whisper evil in the ears of men and turn them mad, further inciting sin and chaos amongst our civilization. The end goal? To give the ultimate "middle-finger" to God, his once master, father, and creator.

Luca looks on in shock as he continues to travel deeper

into the supernatural rabbit hole of the djinn. He gasps as he reads the real life testimonies of other victims of djinn attacks. People talk about hearing or seeing things, others were drained of energy and in the worse cases, some people were completely possessed by these malevolent "spirits".

Shocked and disturbed, Luca slams the laptop shut. Running his hands through his hair, he takes a deep breath and shakes off the chill. That's enough for one night. He dare not tempt "them" anymore, by prying too deep…

* * *

It's a bright but bitterly chilly day, that finds Luca sitting patiently at the local train station platform. He should be over the moon at the return of his girlfriend but he'd rather distract himself by reading a book.

This one is called *"Legend of the Fire Spirits by Robert Lebling"* and is another thesis on the djinn culture and mythology. The chapter he is currently reading deals with link between ghosts, spirits, shapeshifters, the UFO phenomenon and how they all might actually be experiences of djinn visitations.

One interesting piece of information that he circles with a pen, states how all these entities seem to "feed" off of human energy called "loosh". This loosh is a food source for demons and spirits and is more potent in babies, children and teenagers, especially when fueled with adrenaline under stressful situations.

Luca finishes up the last paragraph, folds the corner of the page and closes the book. He takes out his phone and checks the time. It's 2:00PM in the afternoon and there are also a few unopened messages from Arabella.

Luca bites his lip as he contemplates replying. Before he can though, the intercom goes off and signals a train pulling up to the station. Luca switches off his phone and puts it away, standing up to greet the train. It finally comes to a halt at the end of the tracks and all the passengers disembark instantaneously.

Luca stands up awkwardly, book in hand; searching the crowds for a familiar face. Suddenly he spots her, amongst the sea of faces and figures; looking around eagerly for him too. Luca raises his hand and waves. Arabella see's Luca and instantly lights up. They both run to each other, dodging the annoyed passengers along the way.

Finally they beat the tide and embrace in the middle of the platform. Arabella is so excited she jumps up and wraps her legs around Luca's waist. They hold each tight and spin around on the spot before Arabella kisses him on the lips passionately.

"Ah, I've missed you so much!" she shouts. Luca looks around at all the disapproving faces and back at Arabella.

"I missed you too, did you have fun?" he says, gently putting her down.

"Si, certo! My Zio, Alfonso took us truffle hunting out in the forests and when we got back, we cooked and ate them. Oh and then there was the "Festa della Santa Gabrielle", it was stunning! You would have loved it babe. We should go again together sometime!"

Luca nods his head. "Sure, I'd love to!"

The two reunited lovers embrace longingly again, giving no thought to the bumbling citizens brushing past them. Luca tries his best to hug her back the same but his deportment seems off, there is clearly something playing on his mind. They let go of each other and stand apart from one other on the platform.

"So, what you been up to?" Arabella inquires.

Luca puts his book away in his coat pocket and takes Arabella's suitcase from her with one hand. Turning, he gestures for Arabella to follow as he tries to think of a suitable answer.

"Ah nothing much. Just uni and assignments mostly. The usual, you know?"

Arabella catches up and links hands with Luca, who guides them both out of the train station.

"Are you sure you're all right?" prods Arabella, concerned.

Luca looks to Arabella, guiltily.

"Yeah, of course. Why do you say that?"

Arabella shrugs. "Nothing, it's just you don't seem your usual self."

Luca rolls his eyes frustratingly.

"Well nothing's changed, promise. Maybe I'm just tired. I haven't been sleeping well lately with all the insomnia and night-terrors, etc. Also started sniffling the other day, think I might be coming down with something."

Arabella stops and strokes Luca's face. "Aww, mio bambino. Let's get in and out of the cold then!"

Luca smiles and returns the act of comfort. Similarly placing his hand on her cheek too: "Great idea. Come on then, let's get going."

With that, the reunited couple make their way to the bus stop and back to the student halls.

* * *

On their way back, Arabella tells Luca all about her short and unexpected holiday to Italy with her Mum to visit that side of the family. Initially Luca wants to sorn her for going away without letting him know first, but soon decides against it.

In turn, Luca tells her about what he has newly learnt about his sleep paralysis and the djinn. Arabella listens and takes it all in, she is supportive but warns him not to go too deep into it, for his own sanity.

Luca brushes it off and changes the subject, choosing to focus on Arabella instead. After 45 mins, the partners finally arrive back at the student halls. It's late now and the sun has finally set.

Luca takes Arabella's hand and her bags and guides her off the bus, both thanking the bus driver as they depart. Making their way down the path to the crossing, Arabella giggles at Luca's silly jokes and they soon find their footing together again.

They get to the traffic lights and Luca presses the stop button. While they wait, Arabella licks her finger and wipes a small dirt mark off of Luca's cheek.

"Thanks Mum." he teases, as Arabella continues to fuss with an odd curl on Luca's head.

Seeing the lights turn red, Luca brushes her hand away playfully and they turn to cross. As they make their way to the other side, the sky unexpectedly turns from night to day and back again, in the blink of an eye.

The couple immediately shoot a look of shock and confusion at one another. Before they can say anything however, it happens again! Just like that, the sky literally turns from pitch-black to light blue and back again.

Arabella: "Did you see…"

Luca: "Yeah, what the fuck?"

"That was twice!"

Luca looks around and shivers. "Must have been a glitch in the 'Matrix'."

Arabella jabs Luca in the arm. "This isn't funny, that was some weird shit!"

"Sorry babe. I'm just playing."

"Better be…"

They both laugh nervously.

Luca grips Arabella's luggage again and reaches out his hand for her to take.

"Come on, let's get outta here."

Arabella nods and holds Luca's hand, while they both run across the road. As they get to the university hall gates, Luca takes one last look up at the sky. He cannot help but feel like what just happened was a sign. What kind? Who knows. But it leaves Luca with a horrible feeling in the pit of his stomach.

* * *

A few days pass by. Luca and Arabella continue to try and juggle their relationship, friends, hobbies, work, and university. The time they do spend together is good but something has definitely changed between them, and worst of all no one wants to broach the subject for fear of offending the other.

The two ill-fated lovers were both brought up suffering from the same parental traumas and unbeknownst to them found the same energy in each other. A toxic mix if ever there was one. But it is more than that, deep down Luca knows why and soon the truth will come out.

Days turn to weeks and the two try their best to rekindle their romance. Luca paints Arabella's picture, Arabella gifts him a new book, they both make each other mixtapes and learn new cooking recipes. Yet under the surface, things are slowly getting worse.

Arabella loves Luca but she cannot dare introduce him to her father or his side of the family. Their strict Muslim views would not allow it. It is bad enough she does not follow some of the rules herself, let alone if she were to bring home a boy. And a non-Muslim boy at that!

Meanwhile Luca is confused. Arabella wears the Muslim badge with pride but is not extremely selective in what rules she does and does not follow. On top of that, Luca has purposely never engaged with Arabella sexually.

It has always been her who has wanted to do more than kiss and cuddle, although they would not dare have sex. This does not mean Luca does not want it though. He loves her so much and does not how else to express it.

He compliments her, showers her with gifts but it never feels like enough. If it were, surely she would make it official and tell her Dad? Time will surely tell but it may not be the answers either are hoping for.

* * *

One morning, Luca wakes up to the sounds of loud, incessant knocking on his dormitory room door. Rubbing the gunk from his eyes, Luca jumps up and fumbles out of bed.

He sleepily makes his way to the door, tripping on shoes, books, wires and the like. After stubbing his toe twice and wincing in pain, he finally gets to the handle, unlocks the latch and opens the door.

He looks up to see Arabella standing in the hallway, fuming. Her cheeks are puffed up red and her forehead wears a nasty frown that could cut bread. "Hey Babs, you OK?" Luca asks, avoiding her obvious disdain.

"NO!" Arabella screeches, marching past and into Luca's uncharacteristically messy room.

Luca's face goes a pale white in a split second.

"What's up?" he croaks.

"You tell me!"

"I, I...don't know what you mean."

"Think harder. Go on, I'll wait." Arabella snaps ferociously.

"I'm sorry baby, I don't..."

Arabella reaches forward and slaps Luca across the face.

"Don't you call me that!" she yells, tears welling in the corner of her eyes.

Luca just stands there, ashamed. His face drops even further. He has been found out.

"Look. It's not what you think."

Arabella scoffs and looks away. "No, it's probably worse."

Luca looks to the floor and rubs his arm like a child.

Arabella mutters under here breath: "Ibn al Kalb." (Son of a Dog).

Luca hugs himself in shame and tries to explain. "'Bella', it was one night, not even that; a couple of hours. We were both drunk. I was upset after you rejected my request to go official and disappeared on holiday without saying goodbye."

Before he can continue, Arabella slaps him across the face again. Once, twice, three times. Each time getting harder.

Luca blocks the fourth slap. "Stop it! I said I'm sorry OK. It was a mistake. We didn't even have sex."

"Huh, sorry for getting caught more like." Arabella quips, ripping her hand away from Luca.

"It's not like that. I should have been clear with my feelings and waited till you were back to talk. I know that now."

Arabella turns up her face in disgust.

"Whatever, you can keep your dirty little slut! I thought you were different Luca. Did you even mean anything you said to me?"

"Yes! Of course I did, I still do!" Luca pleads.

"Well it doesn't feel like it… it feels like you just waited for me to leave, so you could go and do the dirty."

"No, I didn't plan any of this. It just happened. It was an accident. I didn't know her before and I haven't spoken to her since."

"Haha." Arabella laughs mockingly. "So what? You just *fell* into her, is that it?"

"No."

"Enlighten me then? Go on. I'm waiting."

"I don't, I don't know what to say. I thought I could go without it…"

"What, sex?" Arabella interrupts.

"Yes but it's more than just that. I do love you, more than anyone or anything but you will not introduce me to your Dad, you keep me at arm's length from the rest of your family. You won't make it official. It's been what, seven months now? I thought I would mean more to you., like you mean to me."

"Yeah, well it's a good thing too isn't it?"

"What? Come on… I have given you everything you

asked me for. And more. I haven't held back in anything. I just want the same from you, that's all."

"That's crap Luc, you knew what you were getting into." You knew my position before we started dating... And those excuses don't give you the right to do this!"

"Look Bella, It's not just about sex with you. I want to make love to you. To express how I really feel about you. About us!"

Arabella shakes her head in disbelief.

"Save it. We are over. Why would I want to introduce you to anyone now?"

Arabella heads to the door, shoulder barging Luca on the way.

Luca turns to stop her.

"Arabella, I know I've done wrong but please don't throw us away like this. No one's perfect. Not me or you, not our parents, not anyone! We can all make mistakes in life but that's how we learn."

Arabella stops at the door, hand on the door knob, ready to turn.

"No, this is beyond that. How can I trust you now? I thought we had something real, something special?"

"Argh, we did! We do! It didn't mean a thing. Not like us, I promise…"

"You're full of shit. Tell you what, you like sex so much? Go fuck yourself!"

With that Arabella opens the door, exits and slams it behind her, knocking some books off the shelf next to it. Luca sighs heavily and drops to his knees in the middle of his room. He has no one to blame but himself this time.

He looks around in shame and catches his reflection in the mirror of the darkly lit room. His usually handsome features are now replaced, with something resembling that of the very demonic monsters haunting his dreams.

* * *

Arabella returns to her own halls and throws open her bedroom door. Slamming it shut behind her and jumping onto her bed in a flood of tears, she buries her head into her pillow and lets out a muffled screech. Lifting her head, she wipes her tears with the hoodie she's wearing, creating huge wet marks on her sleeves.

After catching her breath and calming down, Arabella immediately stands up and looks around frantically. Sniffling, she begins to search the room for any and all of Luca's possessions.

Once she has gathered all of his belongings together, Arabella then proceeds to destroy them one by one. She rips up greetings cards, stabs a hole in one his paintings, snaps his mixtape CD's in half and spray paints "CHEAT" on all of his shirts.

Exhausted, Arabella finally stops and assesses the destruction around her. Her heavy breathing slows, her tears run dry and she regains her composure. Opening her draw, she takes out the jar from earlier and smashes it on the desk. The trinkets and jewellery scatter everywhere, revealing her father's ring amongst the debris.

She stares at it for what seems like ages, before picking it up and holding it up to the light. As she examines all its features, she notices something within the black opal that sits encrusted in the middle of the star. It appears to be a moving smokey effect. She squints and leans in to examine it closer. Concentrating harder, she begins to make out a shape within the smoke and her eyes shoot open wide in disbelief.

* * *

The next day finds Luca back at university for a lecture. He couldn't even tell you what the topic of this one is about. He is slouched over his desk, hoody up and one earphone in. His face is perpetually drained, like the lifeforce is slowly being sucked out of him.

His eyes are dark and puffy, like he has not slept for days and his usually well-groomed composure is in tatters. As Luca daydreams, the lecturer makes his way around the room, handing out graded papers to the students. "THUMP" The tutor drops Luca's work over his folded arms and tuts. "What happened Luca. You're better than that."

Luca glances at the marks and sighs, looking away again. The tutor shakes his head and carries on. Mohammed, who is sat a couple of rows back sees the exchange. He looks on and shakes his head too, concerned for his friend.

***

Later that same day, Luca, Shamus and Mohammed are waiting in the lunch queue at the student café. There is a hustle and bustle about the canteen, as students go to and from on what is a surprisingly warm autumn day.

Mohammed pays for his food and heads over to the condiments before taking a seat. Luca is next up and makes his order but when he goes to pay, his card gets declined. Luca asks the for another try and the dinner lady politely agrees but yet again, the card fails.

Sparing Luca further embarrassment, Shamus steps in and offers some cash to pay.

"Nah it's cool, I'll just try the cashpoint." Luca refuses, waving his hand.

"Don't be stupid. Use this, pay me back later." Shamus insists.

Luca pauses for thought, the line of customers growing increasingly annoyed.

Luca finally relents. "You sure? OK man, cheers. I'll sort you out later…"

"Yeah, no worries man." Reiterates Shamus, tapping Luca on the shoulder.

The cashier looks down the line of queuing people and back to Luca. Luca smiles innocently and hands over the cash from Shamus. It is just enough.

Luca takes the change, hands it to Shamus and makes a swift exit to the dinner table where Mohammed is already sat. "All good?" asks Mohammed as Luca takes a seat across from him.

"No but yeah. My card didn't work for some reason. Shamus had to spot me." answers Luca, making himself comfortable.

"Shit." States Mohammed, looking surprised. "Didn't your student finance come through?"

Luca shrugs, frustrated. "Yeah, supposed to."

Shamus finally joins the rest of the gang. "Well that must've been annoying!"

"Sorry man." says Luca.

Shamus shakes his head. "Like I said, no worries. I got you."

Luca smile faintly, humbled. "Thanks again man. I really appreciate it!"

Luca looks off into the middle distance, his pride is hurt but he is genuinely thankful for his friends. Nothing seems to be going right at the moment but he feels like he deserves it.

Whatever the reasoning for someone's actions, there is inevitably always an equal and opposite reaction. Luca is just tasting his own medicine for the first time, and he does not like it. Not one bit. But try as he might, he cannot fight karma and she is a bitch.

* * *

That night and Luca has returned to his room, beaten, and broken; he has suffered the day from hell. He looks and feels like shit, his grades are slipping, his finances are a mess and he may have lost the girl of his dreams.

Luca paces the dormitory bedroom in anxiety, biting his fingers in anticipation. What could be next? Is this his own doing? Is this karma? Or is this something more… sinister. Is this the work of the djinn!

Luca looks around the room frantically, he is muttering to himself; delusional. On his desk, next to his laptop, are his anti-depressant tablets. Once fixated on them, Luca storms over to the table and grabs the bottle.

He picks it up and reads the label, analyzing the ingredients and side effects. After contemplating for a moment, Luca huffs and takes the bottle into the bathroom. He empties the contents of the bottle into the toilet and flushes the chain.

Returning to his room, Luca opens his bedside draw and takes out a small bag of marijuana and his rolling materials. He haphazardly rolls a functioning but unsightly looking joint. He puts a sock over his fire alarm and then lights the spliff.

Inhaling sharp and deeply, Luca moans in satisfaction and slumps into his chair. He takes some more tokes and sighs. Is it possible to feel better and worse at the same time? The weed acts as an eraser, clearing his mind of all the negative, unhealthy thoughts. He has found his new fix.

* * *

Over the next few weeks, Luca slides into a pit of self-destruction. Instead of distracting himself from the pain of heartache with work or studies, he tries to numb the hurt by developing extreme hedonistic tendencies; drinking and smoking until he cannot feel anything anymore.

The song *"Sedated by Hozier"* becomes a frighteningly suitable soundtrack to the start of this particularly dark chapter in is life. Luca meets his dealer more frequently and even starts drinking alone in his dorm room. On top of this, he also finds himself going out more with his flat mates and studying less.

He is soon seen stumbling out of clubs and bars, throwing bottles at a buses when it refuses to pick him up and generally being disruptive and anti-social. It gets to the point where no place wants to let him in and even his friends are starting to wonder what has changed in the guy.

Eventually Luca goes solo, looking for excitement and distraction on his own. One night he ends up in a dingy, dangerous area of town. He knocks on an unmarked door and is greeted by a scantily clad woman, probably a prostitute. She invites him in and the rest as they say, is history.

* * *

At the same time, Arabella is trying to move on with her life, despite that the fact she still cares for and misses Luca.

While waiting outside a classroom one day, she is asked about her relationship by her friends. She shrugs it off and says she is fine and keeping busy. After class, she makes her way to the shuttle bus and checks her phone.

There is a few missed calls and unread messages from Luca. She hovers her thumb over them, while biting her lip, conflicted about responding to him. Before Arabella can decide though, the bus pulls up and instead she pockets the phone and gets on.

* * *

Luca and Arabella have been apart for over three weeks now and tonight finds Luca passed out, depressed, and in bed alone. His desk is scattered with drink bottles and joint roaches and his phone still rests in his hand.

It's left open on some old messages between himself and Arabella; he has fallen asleep whilst reading them, apparently reminiscing on better times. The hour is early in the morning and

Luca's sleep looks restless, ironically much like his waking-life at the moment.

The troubled young man sleeps on, unaware of the particularly nasty critters that are currently stalking him from within the dark recesses of his room. Small, suspiciously-shaped shadows scuttle and scurry around, being careful to avoid any spots of light.

Similarly Luca twists and turns in his bed, subconsciously pulling his quilt tighter around his body with his free hand. At the same time, the temperature is dropping intermittently within the room and with every breath he takes, the more steam that seeps out from of his mouth.

In one corner within the room, a large ball of dark energy builds in size and momentum and approaches Luca's bed. As it passes through the moonlight, the pulsating mass breaks through the veil of the 4th dimension and reveals its true nature.

These particularly nasty entities are like animals of the djinn world and resemble jet-black, spiky tarantulas the size of a small dog. Unfortunately for this would be energy scavenger, it cannot survive in the light and is "burnt" as it attempts to cut across Luca's bedroom floor.

A "line of moonlight" coincidently protects the sleeping Luca from these lower supernatural creatures. Acting like a border-wall and forcing the supernatural spider to retreat quickly back into its corner crevice. Now although Luca's spirit and body are still sleeping, his astral-self is very aware of the astral spiders preying on him from the fourth dimension and so attempts to wake him up.

Back on the physical plane, Luca rolls over onto his side, scratching at his body and perspiring relentlessly. "No, not again..." Luca seems to mutter under his breath, still fast asleep.

The irritation continues, and unable to get comfortable, Luca's eye's flicker open and closed. In the process he glimpses the ghastly insects that literally infest the dark corners of his room (and perhaps metaphorically his mind).

Luca starts to become conscious and controls his eyes, opening and closing them again slowly. Outside his building, the weather takes a turn for the worse and large clouds soon roll in, blocking out any remaining light from the moon.

As Luca continues to focus his vision, a large, stocky figure appears in the centre of his room. It's built like a man but the proportions are all wrong; misshapen and asymmetrical. On its head are foot-long protruding horns that curve up and its body is an inky blend of black & grey shades.

As the figure becomes more visible, so too do the other astral spiders, which even seem to run and hide in fear from this superior, Devil-like entity.

Luca's eye freeze in fixed terror, as the creature moves forward, creating a shadow which reaches out from the middle of his room and crawls across the walls and ceiling towards Luca's bed. With the creatures advancement, so comes a swathe of magnetic energy, which causes Luca's phone to slide from his fingers and thud on the carpet below.

The living shadow reaches Luca's bed and ripples across the sheets, clawing its way through the veil of dimensions. Luca breathes in and out, trying to catch his breath before he passes out. His body is now shaking rapidly, there are sweat patches pooling under his arms and the colour is seeping from his complexion.

Luca closes his eyelids firmly and grits his teeth, praying in desperation. "Get away from me! I'm not afraid of you, God protects me!" he says to himself surely. Curious with Luca's mention of "God", the night-time room invader pauses its attack and circles around Luca's body instead.

The shadow finally groups back into its solid devilish figure and puffs its chest at Luca defiantly.

"That's it, go away! God protects me!" Luca reaffirms. The djinn hesitates once more, vibrating in a state of pure rage and anger at the mention of a holy name. As it vibrates in increasing intensely, so too does its image appear to alter, cycling through a variety of monstrous forms.

Luca senses the creature's defenselessness and throws open the bed covers, sitting up instantly. "You're not welcome here. This soul belongs to Christ. Now leave!" The monster howls and wails, clawing at the space between itself and Luca frantically.

Luca is terrified but knows that he can't back down. He clasps his hands together and prays:

"In the name of the Father, the Son and the Holy-"

The devil djinn has had enough and launches itself forward, attacking Luca in his bed as he prays. Luca opens his eyes to see the face of the demon up close and screams, throwing his hands up in defense just before the point of impact.

And then Luca opens his eyes for real. He's awake now to find himself still tucked up in bed, the phone back in his hand and the monster gone. Luca scans the perimeter, checking and re-checking every nook and cranny.

In the corner of his peripheral vision, Luca notices that his bedroom door is ajar. As he turns his head to investigate more closely, the door suddenly slams shut!

Luca jumps up courageously and runs to the door. He grabs the handle and twists it, but it's either locked or something is holding it shut from the other side. Luca struggles, the door wiggles. "Argh! Come on." Luca yells as he fights back, tugging at the door with all his might.

Suddenly the grip form the other side releases and the door flies open, almost sending Luca flying off of his feet. Luca manages to brace himself and plants his heels firmly into the carpet. Pulling himself forward, he lunges out of the room and into the hallway.

At the other end of the flat, a large, dark mass in the shape of a humanoid figure, looks back at Luca malevolently, before turning and gliding away into the dark.

Luca, eyes wide in disbelief, looks around to the other bedroom doors. They are all shut and with their light's off. No one's awake. Cautiously, Luca follows the direction of the creature, about 10 feet down the hallway and around the corner to the stairs, where he sees:

The Djinn, different from the one in his room, standing right in front him; no more than two feet away. It towers Seven or eight feet tall, poised and ready to attack. Its claws protrude from its decomposing fingers and its spiny, snarling teeth shine like icicles or stalactites.

What frightens Luca the most though are its eyes. Big, red, and bloody like a fiery eclipse, their intensity burns a hole right through Luca's being.

Then without warning the djinn lunges at Luca, screeching like a heathen and extending its mouth wide ready to consume him. Taken by surprise, Luca drops his hands to his sides and whispers. "Forgive me God. Forgive me Bella."

And just like that Luca wakes up. He's back in his bed, mobile phone still in hand; everything exactly as it should be. Was that a nightmare? A dream? It felt so real! It was real, wasn't it? Luca scratches his head, bemused and in shock.

Luca pinches himself to check if he might still be dreaming but winces immediately upon feeling the pain. He then goes to check the time on his phone and catches his face in the screen reflection. He turns his nose up in disgust, barely recognising the tired and snow pale person looking back at him.

Looking immediately around him, Luca realises that his sheets are crumpled and soaked in sweat. Darting his head around the room, Luca searches for something, anything; to validate what just happened. Alas he is alone and there's no evidence of anyone in the room now or prior. He's safe. For now at least it would seem…

"Awakening is not changing who you are but discarding who you are not."

ACCURSED

Chapter 5

Arraigned

A waitressing exchange-student, is clearing tables in a dimly-lit, Italian restaurant in central London. It has been a few months now since Luca and Arabella first split up. After going their own separate ways for a while, they eventually reached out to one another again, in the hopes of getting some closure.

It's almost closing time now and the premises is near

empty, save for an awkward looking couple tucked away in the very back corner. The couple is Luca and Arabella, sitting anxiously across the table from one another, wondering if this reunion was a good idea after all.

Luca piques up first and tries to break the ice. "So, how's your uni assignments going?"

Arabella, still refusing to make eye contact; shrugs and looks out the window. "Fine." She responds coldly.

Luca clears his throat. "I really do miss you; you know?"

"Shame you didn't miss me before, while I was away on holiday..." she scolds, meeting his gaze for the first time.

Luca looks away, embarrassed. "I'm so sorry. That was totally out of order. I know that. I instantly regretted it-"

Arabella rolls her eyes, fed up.

"You remember the first day we met? When I saw you at that social party?" Luca continues.

Arabella drops her guards, just a little, thinking back to how it all began.

"Remember what I said to you?"

Arabella's shoulders relax, she looks around the restaurant.

"Sei ancora la ragazza piu bell ache abbia mai visto!" (You are still the most beautiful girl I have ever seen).

Arabella slips a sly smile and then returns to frowning. "Then why do it? Huh? If all that's so true, why cheat?"

Luca stutters. He is not sure what to say. The truth might hurt her even more. He decides it is best to be as honest as possible, even if it might not be what she wants to hear at first. Luca clears his throat and straightens up in his seat.

"A moment of weakness, I was lonely. You left unexpectedly and without a proper goodbye. I asked to be with you the day before you left. Offered to help you pack and everything. So all that combined with you rejecting my offer to go steady, I thought you weren't serious. I mean, you have met my Dad already, spoke to my family. I barely know of yours!"

Arabella scoffs.

"Look, I just want to love and feel love back in a relationship. We are supposed to be together. I just want to be able to express that. I want it to be with you, not some random girl."

Arabella shakes her head, still at a loss for words but she tries to hear him out.

Luca: "I was a late bloomer, you know this. In fact, when it came to girls, I was a "nerd" at school. I never even knew how to speak to girls and when I tried, always got shot down. Now I come to uni; to London. I've more confident, I've grown into myself and my features and it is a totally different story. I wasn't ready for it…"

Arabella starts to play with her cutlery, clearly agitated about the topic of the conversation.

"On top of that, although I was brought up Catholic, sex has never really been taboo… as long as it is safe and legal of course. This celibacy idea is new to me. I've never had Muslim friends or family before coming here, and certainly no lovers. It's harder to adapt than I first thought. Especially when it's you instigate all the other sexual activity between us."

Arabella throws the cutlery down on the table.

"I don't see the big deal, it's just sex!"

"Yes but it could be so much more too. The ultimate expression of love between two people. When you experience it for the first time, you'll understand."

"Don't patronize me Luca. Why did you ask me here?"

Luca readies himself. He knows he is asking a lot.

"I... I want you to give us a second chance. I know it's not been the best of starts but with time we could be so good together. A real power couple."

Luca takes a breath and gulps.

"I mean, imagine how good looking our kids would be!"

Arabella smiles fractionally at the thought but swiftly tries to hide any tell-tale signs with her hand.

"No rush, just take things slow. Start again... as friends first?" Luca adds.

"They would be gorgeous... and just think of their hair too!" Arabella states.

"So, what do you say?"

Arabella ponders for a moment. At the same time, Luca reaches over and takes her trembling hand, his eyes welling up.

"Please? You're the best thing that's happened to me."

Arabella bites her lip and pulls her hand away. She sits back in her chair and fiddles with her nails.

Luca looks on, hopeful, wiping the wet from his cheeks. He does not blink, awaiting Luca's response patiently.

Arabella: "I dunno Luca. I can't get hurt again. Not like that."

Luca: "You won't!"

"I'm gonna need time, to think about it; to think about everything."

Luca's eyes light up. "Of course, that's all I ask!"

Arabella looks away from Luca and out through their reflections in the restaurant window. Rain drops begin to spatter on the glass. She wonders if it's an omen, if she's just marked her own demise but alas Arabella relents. Despite the hurt, despite his lies, she has a feeling deep down that there's still more to their story.

Meanwhile Luca stares on at Arabella, taking in every line, every freckle, every curve and wonders if this is the last time he will ever get to see these uniquely beautiful features. Only time will tell.

* * *

Over the next couple of months Luca and Arabella attempt a life again as some sort of couple. They take things back to basics, beginning at first as friends, then gradually getting more serious like they had before.

They go on walks and bike rides in the park together, read books by the river, exercise in the park and even attempt to play basketball together. Luca tries to take more of an interest in Arabella's religion and wakes up with her to watch her pray; sometimes even meditating alongside her at the same time. As they try their best to heal the wounds of the past, they also reveal more intimate sides of themselves to each other.

Luca was one of three siblings and often felt left out and insecure, like he was never quite "good enough". Arabella can relate too as although she did not have siblings, her parent's relationship was toxic and focused on them, not her. Luca opens up about suffering from depression as a teen and being on and off medication. They agree to help each other and try to understand one another's flaws as best they can.

Time goes on and they explore new things together; shopping, cinema's, shisha bars; even a trips abroad to Europe and North Africa. Luca professes his love and suggests running away together and getting married. Arabella, typically, laughs it off.

Unnerved at her response, Luca pretends to mimic her amusement but deep down he is heartbroken. Little does he know however; Arabella doesn't see how it could possibly work long term and is starting to accept that he probably isn't the one for her. For now though, she is willing to see where it can go.

And maybe she is right too. Maybe this is a car crash in slow motion. Maybe these two characters, from two vastly different backgrounds, just aren't meant to be together in this lifetime. Only passing ships in the night, trading experiences, memories and lessons learned. If only this temporary union didn't have to be so painful.

* * *

One winter's night, later that year, Luca and Arabella exit a shisha bar called "She-sha Lounge". The couple are in Arabella's hometown, while on a break from university. She is finally letting Luca in a bit more and has introduced him to parts of her mother's side of the family.

Although much to his frustration, her father's side is still a mystery. And as they are soon to find out, probably with good reason. Arabella takes a sip of Rio and hooks her arm underneath Luca's, the sounds of high street and late night revelers echoing in the background.

Stepping off the curb, the couple head across the road and round the corner to the taxi ranks. As they cross again and make another left, they come across another, older couple heading in the opposite direction. Arabella looks away from Luca, laughing at a joke, when she recognizes the man as her father, Khalid.

"Shit!" Arabella stammers, turning back to Luca.

"What is it?" asks Luca, confused.

"It's my bloody Dad…"

"Where? Oh- ."

Before Luca can finish his sentence, Khalid is already heading towards Arabella smiling, an unknown women trailing a couple of metres behind him. As they approach, Luca notices

Khalid quickly stub out a cigarette and throw it away. The woman continues to smoke hers.

"Arabella, how are you my baby." Khalid yells, throwing open his arms.

"Hey Papa, I'm good..." Arabella answers, hugging Khalid back. She slyly turns her nose up at the smell of nicotine. Khalid still sports the same wiry frame from when he was a child. Only he is taller now, with a lighter complexion and a goatee beard.

He is dressed in an expensive suit and his lady companion is in a tight black dress. His eyes are bloodshot and the smell of alcohol emanates from his aura. After catching up with his estranged daughter, Khalid looks over to Luca and gestures.

"Who's this? Aren't you going to introduce us?"

Arabella looks at Luca awkwardly, then quickly masks it with a smile. Luca takes the initiative and reaches out his hand to Khalid.

Luca: "Hi Mr. Abboud, I'm-"

Before he can finish however Arabella quickly interjects. "This is my friend, Luca. From uni."

Luca's face drops for a split second. That was not the introduction he was expecting. But then again, this was not the end to the night he was expecting either. Luca brushes it off and shakes Khalid's hand.

"Hello Luca."

"Nice to meet you, sir."

"I hope you're taking care of my daughter?"

"Of course Mr. Abboud. In fact I was just taking her to the taxi rank now."

"Good man. Do not get any funny ideas with her eh? Haha!"

"Uh, of cours-"

Again Arabella intervenes before Luca can finish.

Arabella: "Uh, he's gay Dad. No need to worry about that."

Luca is hurt. It is one thing to pretend they are not an item. It is another to just make up lies. Luca bites his tongue, though, he knows she has her reasons.

Khalid laughs at Arabella's comment.

"Ah well, no worries there then. Haha!"

Arabella decides to move the conversation on.

"And who's this? Sorry, I didn't get your name?" she questions, finally acknowledging the woman Khalid is with.

The lady steps forward from behind Khalid. She is a lot younger than him and maybe only a few years older than Arabella. By the styling of her make-up and clothes, one might assume she were a lady of the night.

Khalid: "Oh yes, right! This is Anastasia, my business partner."

Anastasia offers up her hand to Arabella and speaks in a thick Eastern European accent.

"Hello, nice to meet you."

Arabella clears her throat. "Hi, nice to meet you too."

Luca nods from the side, growing increasingly uncomfortable.

"Anyways, you better be getting home and to bed "Bella". It's late!" Khalid imposes.

Arabella looks to Luca embarrassingly and back to her father. "Yes papa, we're going now."

Luca nods to Khalid and Anastasia and starts to move on. Arabella hugs her Dad and waves at his new girlfriend halfheartedly. "Bye Luca. Keep my daughter out of trouble… or else!"

Luca humours the man and continues on his way. "I will, don't worry!"

With that, the two couples walk in opposite directions and disappear again, like ships in the night.

As they continue on their way, Luca turns to Arabella. "Well that was awkward!"

"Sssh." Insists Arabella, pushing her finger to her lips.

"They can't hear us. Besides, they're probably saying the exact same thing."

Arabella nudges Luca sharply in the rib.

"Oww, I'm only playing." Luca moans, rubbing delicately at his side.

"Look I don't think that's the introduction anyone wanted." Arabella shrugs, before returning to Luca's side.

"I guess not. So who was that lady anyway?"

Arabella looks to the floor. "I'm really not sure."

"Not his girlfriend then, huh?"

"Not exactly…"

Luca looks confused. "Wait, what do you mean?

"Well I think she's a djinn."

Luca, shocked now: "What! A djinn?"

"When I was younger and my parents were splitting up, I always used to see her about. My Dad used to say she was a family friend but I always got these weird vibes from her."

Luca throws his hands up. "Thank God it wasn't just me! I thought it might have been drink or drugs but maybe she's just soul-less?"

"No, she's always been cold like that; anytime I've met her. She's like a robot, right? It's funny, My Dad told me when he was a kid that he had a friend, a girl, that was like a "guardian angel" helping him out when he was stuck. Bringing him good luck, etc. Maybe it's the same person?"

"Or thing…" Luca corrects.

The two look at each other anxiously.

"Damn, that's heavy." Luca states.

"I know. Welcome to my life." replies Arabella.

As the couple continue on down the road to the taxi ranks, Luca takes one final glance back. As he does, he just about makes out Khalid and Anastasia about to turn a corner. As he stares, Anastasia suddenly turns around and glares back at him!

Her eyes flash blood red and a malicious grin creeps across her face, chilling Luca to his bones. Luca quickly turns back-around and grabs Arabella's hand. They speed up to the taxi ranks and hastily hail a cab.

* * *

The half term holidays are over and students are back to class as normal. One day during the evening, flat mates Luca, Tim and Shamus are all chilling together in the living area. Tim and Shamus are playing FIFA on the PlayStation, whilst Luca sits around the dining table, text books and notepad open.

He is trying to crack a tough assignment but is instead finding himself thinking about Arabella, her Father, and their relationship. Luca checks his phone repeatedly but there are no messages. Since that night back in Arabella's home town, she has been quiet; distant.

"Go on the boys!" screams Shamus as he scores a goal against Tim.

"What the fuck was he doing? Just let you dribble straight past him."

"Haha, you know what they say about bad work men!"

"Come on, you bloody saw that! I pressed the button like ten times."

"Did you see that?" Shamus shouts over to Luca.

"Uh, yeah, sure..." offers Luca, half listening.

"Hello? Earth to Luca?" Shamus mocks, pausing the game.

"Leave him man. Probably daydreaming over that girl of his again!" adds Tim.

"No!" exclaims Luca. "Well yeah, kinda..."

"So what's the story? You two done it yet?" asks Shamus unashamedly.

Luca shakes his head and looks back to his text books.

Shamus: "Damn."

Tim: "You're a stronger man than most! Haha."

Shamus puts down his controller and joins Luca at the table. "So, how long's that now?" he questions Luca.

"How long's what?" Luca asks.

"Your dick!" jokes Shamus. "No. How long you been without sex you ejit!"

Luca rolls his eyes, getting it now.

"Too long, I guess." he answers.

Tim and Shamus laugh at his response. Luca forces a smile but doesn't think his relationship is a joke.

Tim carries on. "I couldn't do it man. I mean you gotta go through all the bullshit of a relationship but without the reward?"

"Yeah, not really fair is it?" says Shamus.

Luca: "Maybe not but I reckon she's worth it."

"Yeah, OK that's what they all say." remarks Tim.

"Yeah, give it time…" states Shamus.

Luca is frustrated now. He knows they are probably only joking but it still hurts. He just wants a normal relationship like everyone else. He sees Tim with his girlfriend, he sees his sister

Tatiana with her boyfriend, he sees all these other couples around him.

They all are open and committed, have introduced parents to one another, and seem generally happy, not just sexually. Why is this relationship; his relationship, so different?

"No, it's what I say, no one else. Because I know her and I'm into her. Sex isn't everything. Alright?"

Shamus and Tim look to one another and back at Luca and instantaneously burst out laughing.

Tim: "Haha, all right, touchy!"

Shamus: "Yeah, chill! We're just playing with yah!"

Luca closes his textbooks and notepads and clears the kitchen table. "Ah forget about it." He mumbles as the boys continue to laugh. Tim holds up his PlayStation controller. "Another game?"

Shamus returns to the living room and picks up his controller too. "OK but I'm Barca this time!" Luca gets up and leaves the dining area, contemplating their conversation and his situation as a whole. As he makes his way upstairs to his room, the other lads continue with their gaming.

* * *

Another couple of weeks pass and Luca finds himself banging angrily on the door of Arabella's student house. In his spare hand he has his phone to his ear, seemingly trying to get hold of her that way too.

"Come on, come on. Pick up." He mutters as he paces outside the front porch. Frustrated, he looks around for signs of life but the streets are empty. Luca does spot a nosy older neighbour peeking through a curtain but does not let it stress him.

Luca calls again. The phone rings. "Come on "Bells". Answer..." he pleads. Luca goes to bang the front door but before his first can connect, it opens and he almost hits Arabella's flat mate in the chest. At the same time, the phone line on his mobile goes dead. Good timing he thinks.

Luca puts the mobile away and fixes himself up before opening his mouth. "Hi, Teresa? Right?" greets Luca, waving his hand by.

"No. Elisa." Arabella's flat mate responds, plainly.

"Oops, my bad."

"What do you want Luca?" Elisa interjects. "I got a stinking hangover. I wanna sleep…"

"I'm really sorry but have you seen Bella?"

"She's out."

"Out where?" Luca says, holding up his phone. "I can't get hold of her by phone. And she's been flaky for weeks."

"Chill man. She's with her Dad. They're spending some time together, trying to reconnect."

Luca goes silent, he does not know what to say. Why couldn't Arabella tell him this.

Luca: "OK cool. No worries "El" and thanks."

Elisa: ""El" now is it?"

"Can you tell Bella that I've popped home for a few days to the family and run some errands. When you see her, that is."

Elisa looks around the neighbourhood and back to Luca.

"Sure, but you'll probably speak to her first."

"Thanks so much. I gotta go catch my bus. I'll see you round."

"Yeah , see yah…"

Luca leaves in a hurry, picking up his small suitcase on the way.

*　*　*

After hours on the road, Luca's bus pulls into Bristol coach station. As it grinds to a halt, the rumble of the engine shutting off wakes Luca up. He was napping against the window, using his own hoody as a makeshift pillow.

As the other passengers filter off, Luca gathers up his things and check his mobile: there is still no reply from Arabella. He sighs to himself and continues to disembark from the bus.

Wasting no time, Luca leaves the station and makes his way over to the taxi ranks. There are no cars available at the moment, so he props up his luggage and sits on top of the suitcase. After getting comfortable, Luca then gets out his phone and searches for an available cab number.

Just as he is about to press call on a suitable company, he notices a girl waving at him from the other side of the bay. As she approaches, Luca begins to recognize her. "Hey!" she squeals, bouncing over to Luca.

"Oh hey... Becca right?" Luca responds, putting his phone away.

"Yeah, Tatianna's friend from school." Becca replies.

"Oh wow. You're older!"

"Yup, time will do that. Haha!"

"Yeah, true. Hehe."

Becca opens her arms and invites Luca for a hug. The two embrace momentarily. "So how are you?" Becca asks.

"I'm not too bad thanks, yourself?" responds Luca.

"Yeah, great thanks! Just back for a few weeks to see the fam."

"Oh cool, me too actually!"

Becca rests her bags and shopping next to Luca's and they continue to converse in the cool night air.

"So, you're still at uni right?" Becca asks.

"That's right, finishing my second year now. Going into my third."

"Ah well done! I, uh, dropped out..." admits Becca.

"Aw how come?" says Luca sincerely.

Becca looks uncomfortable. She tucks back her hair and smacks her lips. "Just wasn't right for me, you know. I'm still doing music though and recording a new EP soon. So it's all good."

Luca smiles reassuringly. "That's good. I'm glad. Your voice is amazing!"

"Yeah. And plus I am working part time in this vegan shop for extra "moolah" in the meantime!"

"Man, I wish I had the balls to do that. Ever since year one I wasn't sure this course was for me. But I'm too far in now and have spent far too much!"

"Right? It's extortionate! University should be a privilege, not a product!

Luca laughs. "Tell me about it. I'm 15K down already…"

"Ouch!" states Becca, wincing at the thought.

"Ouch is right." agrees Luca.

Then it all goes quiet for a moment. They both look around and realise how deserted the town is. Luca goes to get his phone out again when Becca leans in: "Hey, so my bus isn't due for another half hour. You wanna grab a coffee quick or something?"

Luca stops mid-action, surprised. He pauses, thinking about the time, Arabella and getting up early tomorrow.

"Come on. It has been ages! I won't keep you long..." Becca urges.

Luca looks at the taxi rank and sees no cabs have turned up. He looks back to Becca and smiles. "Um, OK, sure. One coffee!"

* * *

A few minutes later and the two old friends find themselves in the local travel café. Luca is sat at a table near a window, checking his phone. He finally has a response from Arabella, asking how he is, where he is and what he's up to.

Luca rolls his eyes. He hasn't been able to get hold of her in days and now she messages out of the blue and with no explanation. He reads it again and goes to reply. But just as he begins, Becca returns from the café counter with drinks and cakes.

Becca: "Et voila! Two soya lattes."

Luca: "Merci beacoup!"

"D'eren."

Luca immediately picks up his coffee and blows on it. "So…"

Becca does the same. "So. You still into your spiritualism?"

"Sure! I mean, not as much as I used to be. It's kind of taken a back seat with uni and stuff. I go through phases… haha."

"That's fair enough. I'm the same really. I've found going vegan really helped though."

"Oh yeah? I've been slowly cutting out the bad stuff too. Would be nice to go full on at some point though."

"No rush, all in good time."

"True." Luca ponders. "I've trying to cleanse my chakras actually. You know, purify the mind… and body."

"Good idea. I can give you some tips. Plus, doing that will certainly help with your creativity and studies."

Luca nods. "Very true, a huge bonus but not the main reason I am doing it."

"Oh yeah?" Becca leads.

Luca pauses, debating whether he should even be telling her this. He glances at the time on a clock on the wall. They have only been here five minutes. He takes a deep breath and hunches in closer.

"Yeah, so I've been having these night terrors or "sleep paralysis"" as they call it. So I will go to bed, get off to sleep and then suddenly when it gets to early/mid-morning have these terrible nightmares. Sometimes I wake from these bad dreams but I am paralysed; I can see but not move. And then there is this presence, this evil energy, that's there in the room with me!"

Becca eyes widen in shock at Luca's story, yet she can't help but be equally fascinated by it.

"That's intense!" She finally replies, before inquiring further: "So how often does this happen? And what does this "thing" even want?" she questions.

"Well it comes and goes, like in phases. But when it does happen, it can last up to two or three times a week." Luca replies.

"And the "thing" that's there with you, what is it?"

"No idea. Lots of people say lots of different things. Aliens, boogeymen, black-hats, ghosts… djinn."

"Do they say or do anything to you?"

"No discussions yet. In fact, I'm not sure they *can* talk." Luca looks around the café. There are other customers but no one close enough to hear their private and probably alarming conversation. He continues.

"Sometimes they stand there, at the end of the bed. Other times they sit. But they're always watching, judging, hating. It feels like they're big cats, stalking, and I'm the prey."

"Bloody hell that is spooky. Hehe. Have you looked into it much? I've not heard of it before you see."

"Of course. There are many theories though. Some people think it is all just an overabundance of DMT, seeping over from the dream-state while you're waking up. Other, crazier theories suggest they are actually "Greys", alien visitors who abduct and experiment on humans. Then again, they could be hallucinations too… I am bipolar after all. Haha."

"Don't say that." Becca asserts strongly.

"Sorry." He quickly responds.

Becca takes a sip of her drink, processing Luca's story fully. "And what do you think?" she asks.

"Me? Well I keep getting drawn back to the djinn theory. Just seems to make the most sense to me. Also it's the most documented and widely believed of all the theories currently out there. Heck David Icke even talks about them in his lectures"

"Djinn theory?" repeats Becca.

"Yeah, so my friend at uni is Muslim. He says that in Islam they talk about the djinn all the time, as a matter of *fact*."

Becca looks confused still. Luca explains.

"So the djinn are a race of creatures apparently created by God, before man. They live here on earth but on another plane of existence, or dimension if you will. When we sleep, we are able to crossover into their dimensions using our astral bodies. Likewise, they too sometimes cross over onto our plane."

Becca cups her chin in her hands and leans into meet Luca, fascinated now.

"And what do they look like exactly?"

"Well to us they appear as these tall, mostly black, humanoid creatures that move like smoke. Supposedly they can shape shift too. Oh and the ones I've seen had glowing red, sometimes yellow eyes…"

"Gosh, this all sounds so scary. Have you seen them lately?"

"No, not for a little while now. They've been "quiet" recently. Haha!"

"And your girlfriend, what does she think?"

"Well she's Muslim as well actually. She's heard of them too and understands it all but I'm not totally sure that she actually believes me."

"Well it all sounds pretty convincing to me. Besides, why would you make this up?"

"Thanks and yeah, exactly!"

"How does your relationship fare with all that?"

Luca is a bit taken back at the question but obliges Becca. "Ah, we're all right. We have our ups and downs like most people but we're good."

"You don't seem so certain."

"It's not that, it just has its difficulties. Like any other relationship."

"Like what?"

"I dunno, it can be a bit difficult with the culture difference and religion, etc. I love being with her and can see a future with her but I'm not so sure that she does with me. It's always on her terms, in her time."

"Explain." Becca encourages.

Luca pauses and glances around the café again. There are less people than before. He looks to the clock again, too. They have another twelve minutes before her coach supposedly gets in to the station.

Luca: "Well we only recently made it official but still not "official-official" because most of her family don't even know. She can't tell them because I'm not Muslim. Also we can't have sex, obviously and anything intimate is always initiated by her. Which is fair but I somehow feel left out. On top of all that, she can be quite demanded about what I can and can't do, etc."

"Well that kinda sucks. Thought relationships were supposed to be a two way thing, you know?"

Luca shrugs slightly and throws his hands up.

"Go figure!"

"I dunno. I couldn't be in a relationship like that. You are supposed to grow closer over time, not keep each other at arm's length. Why don't you tell her what you really want. Speak honestly?"

"I have. She either doesn't wanna listen or digs her heels in harder. There's no winning that battle."

"She doesn't know what she's missing Luc."

Then, Becca reaches out a hand and touches Luca's. She leans in even closer and looks him in the eye. Luca smiles awkwardly and gently pulls his hand away. Becca sits back in her chair, smiles, and bites her bottom lip.

"I wouldn't let you go to waste like that." She slips suggestively.

Luca coughs and sits back in his chair, somewhat embarrassed. Looking for a distraction, he raises his hand and calls a waiter for the bill.

An employee spots his request and nods from across the café, motioning "one minute" with his finger. Contented, Luca returns to Becca who is now checking her make-up in a hand-held mirror. She catches Luca looking and winks back at him flirtatiously.

Becca: "Shame we'll never find out eh?"

* * *

Luca wakes up the next day, back home at his parents' house. He is groggy, grumpy and has a headache like a hangover. Even the comfort of his own childhood bed is not enough to put him in a good mood this morning.

Luca sits up in his bed and contemplates for a second. He turns and looks to the empty space next to him; he wishes it were Arabella who were sleeping next to him. He thinks harder, recollecting the prior night before; meeting Becca, getting coffee and then after…

Luca facepalms himself with both hands and moans in disappointment. He looks out to the window and shakes his head. He did not sleep with Becca but entertaining her was bad enough. As Luca motivates himself to get up, his phone beeps on top of the bedside cabinet. Luca picks it up and checks the messages. There is another one from Arabella asking where he is and that she's worried.

Scrolling through the other notifications, Luca soon sees more unread messages; including one from Becca. He sighs in frustration and reluctantly checks her message too. It reads: "Hey, had so much fun last night. Take care and don't be a stranger!"

Luca throws the phone face down on the bed and then shoves his head into his pillow and screams. "Vaffanculo" he mumbles to himself, punching the headboard.

After taking a beat to cool off, Luca jumps up and heads straight to the door. As he passes his bedroom mirror, he catches something in the reflection. Pausing briefly to check himself out, Luca examines his bloodshot, tired eyes and the newfound stubble on his chin. He frowns in disgust and quickly carries on. But as he leaves, a dark figure moves menacingly in the background of the room. Its blood red eyes twinkling at Luca, always watching from within the darkness.

* * *

After freshening up, Luca heads outside for a morning coffee and cigarette. He slides open the patio door and steps outside into the garden. He has a hand rolled cigarette in one hand and a lighter in the other. He finds a spot down and around the side of the house, props his foot up against the brick wall and lights the cigarette. Luca takes a long drag and inhales deeply.

He enjoys that first toke and closes his eyes. For a moment he forgets about it all. Uni, his assignments, his future, his relationships and most importantly all his problems. Luca breathes out and opens his eyes; remembering it all again.

As he continues to smoke, his phone beeps in his pocket. He retrieves it promptly and sees it's another message from Arabella: "Hey baby, worried about you. Sorry I went quiet. Had a surprise visit from my Dad. Message me!"

Luca sighs and takes another toke. He ponders on the message and finally plucks up the courage to reply. He texts back: "Ciao Bella. I'm Ok thanks. Just got back late, knackered! Will call you soon. X"

Reading it over again, he nods to himself in approval, presses send and puts the phone back in his pocket. As he does, he notices the flash of a large, dark shadow in his peripheral vision. Luca looks back in the same direction but curiously, nothing is there now.

Scanning the alleyway again and the garden beyond it, Luca shivers as a cold feeling runs down his spine.

He strains his eyes again, trying to make out what could have possibly caused the movement. Then he notices it. A small black and white cat perched between two plant pots; just sitting there, staring directly at him. Its eyes are wide open and hypnotic. Luca stares back at the cat for a good few second's and then stamps his foot unexpectedly and "Shoos" it away.

The cat does not budge. Then Luca notices something unnerving; there are two other cats watching him as well. One is sat, crouched on the neighbours bordering wall and the other is led on top of the fence at the end of the garden. Luca looks around to see if anyone is watching; he is alone. He rests what is left of the roll up in his mouth and chases after the cats, picking up a broom as he goes.

The cats promptly jump up and scatter in different directions. Angry now, Luca throws the broom after them aimlessly, dropping the fag in the process. "That's right, piss off!" Luca shouts, while scooping up a handful of stones. He pivots on the spot and pelts the stones in various directions. But the cats are already long gone and Luca is left standing alone like an idiot.

He looks around the back gardens of the neighboring houses once more but again, there's no sign of anyone. Luca straightens his clothes and brushes back his hair, returning to his original smoking spot. As he walks, Luca picks up the rest of his fag-end on the way and frequently glances back over his shoulder.

As he does, he catches glimpse of a tall, voluptuous feminine figure in the corner of his periphery. Turning to witness the miracle fully, Luca is marveled by this elemental femme fatale. She is floating about three feet off the ground and seems to bellow in the wind, as if she were made of fire or water.

Luca freezes, dropping the cigarette again. He blinks in disbelief, startled by this Amazonian figure in his back garden. The "goddess" dazzles Luca for a few more seconds before the sound of a car pulling up distracts his attention.

Half-turning to find out who has arrived, Luca is almost blinded, when she bursts into a magnificent multitude of colours and then evaporates.

***

A few days later and Luca returns to university. He surprises Arabella late that night by going to hers straight from the coach station. She greets him at the door and tells him he is just in time for dinner. After disposing of his luggage, Luca joins Arabella in her student-accommodation kitchen, while she continues to cook.

"Allora, mio bello!" (Well then my beautiful) Arabella says while cutting some vegetables. "How are your parents, and everyone else?"

Luca goes over to the sink and washes his hands. "They're good thanks, taking it easy." Luca then takes another, small knife from the stand and starts to prepare the chicken meat. "And my sisters are good too. They all say hey!"

Arabella starts to dice the veg into smaller chunks. "That's good, I'm glad."

"Yeah, I really am lucky to have them."

Arabella scoops up all the diced food into a bowl and wipes down the work surface. At the same time, Luca proceeds to season the meat with a variety of herbs and spices.

Arabella: "I missed you, you know. And I'm sorry again about my Dad. He does that from time to time. Just drop in unannounced."

Luca nods. "It's fine, I get it. Just wish I could be part of that side of your life more."

Arabella smiles and leans over to peck Luca on the lips. "You will, one day."

The couple brush noses and then return to their tasks.

"So, chef! What are we making?" Luca questions.

"Stir fry, your favourite!" squeals Arabella.

Luca raises his eyebrows and licks his lips. "Mm, yu-"

Luca is halted mid-sentence by the unexplainable sound of footsteps from directly above the kitchen.

Arabella hears the noise too and also freezes from her task, the pair looking to each other for reassurance.

Luca: "No one's in, right?"

Arabella: "No! 100%! Elisa is at her boyfriends. Jodi is back home and Marni and Niamh are ou-."

Again the pitter-patter of footsteps interrupt Arabella mid-flow. The couple look up to the ceiling and back down at each other.

"OK, what the actual fuck!" Arabella shouts.

"Chill." says Luca calmly. "Stay here and I'll go have a look."

"No, I wanna come with you." pleads Arabella.

Luca smiles encouragingly and gestures to Arabella to get behind him. "You definitely heard that right?" She persists.

"Unfortunately, yes Bella."

"Do you think it was a djinn?"

"I bloody hope not. Besides, I thought you said not to talk about that?"

"OK, forget I sa-"

"CRASH!" Out of nowhere, the knives stand on top of the window ledge comes smashing to the floor. Steel and plastic clank and clatter across the tiles, just missing Luca and Arabella's feet by inches. Both of them jump and scream in fright and immediately rush out of the kitchen.

* * *

That same night, Luca and Arabella lay awkwardly on Luca's, back at his student flat. The couple were so spooked by what happened at Arabella's place, that they decided to get out altogether. The television is playing an old 1980's horror film called *"Wishmaster"* (a western take on the evil genie mythos) but they're both too tired now to pay any attention.

Around them on the bed are empty Chinese takeaway food boxes and used fizzy pop cans. Luca, who is already half asleep, decides to clean up the mess so they can call it a night. As he does, Arabella begins to get changed into her night clothes. While doing so, she becomes aware of a new poster on Luca's bedroom wall.

"That's a cool poster, when did you get that?" Arabella asks, pointing to entrancing image of a woman in a head scarf, walking in the middle of a sand storm, looking head on at the photographer.

"Oh that?" Luca reaffirms, looking up at the poster in question. "That was a gift from Mohammed."

"Huh... really..."

"Yeah, he said he had two copies so decided to give me one. Cool right?"

Arabella looks forlorn. Now fully changed into her night clothes, she walks over to the wall where the poster is. She assesses it closely for a moment and then turns to Luca: "Do you think Mohammed could be jealous or envious of you?"

"What do you mean? Why would you say that?"

Arabella returns to the bedside and helps Luca clear up. "Well, I mean he does come out with some weird things sometimes. The way I catch him looking at you... no, *staring* at you even; is creepy."

"Sure he can be a little odd at times." Luca answers.

"I'm sure he's on the spectrum or something..."

"Well maybe but that doesn't mean he's up to no good!"

"I know, I'm not saying that Luc."

Luca is getting a little impatient and audibly huffs, unsure of where exactly Arabella is going with this.

She eventually explains: "I'm just saying: be careful! I mean, you never really know someone. And this guy is from the

North Africa too right. He knows about djinn, evil eye, curses, spells; all of that!"

Luca is surprised and taken aback. "You can't be serious?"

"Totally. It's not unheard of for people to put a bad spell on someone they feel threatened by. Or send them the "Evil Eye"."

Luca scratches his head and blows a raspberry. "Well the poster was really out of the blue and not like him at all. Plus, now that I think of it; I do seem to have more sleep paralysis episodes after I've spent time with him."

Arabella gets up again and returns to the poster. She runs her hands across it inquisitively and glances at Luca: "We should burn it!"

"What? No! That was a gift Bella…"

Arabella just shrugs and folds her arms. "That's the only way to get rid of evil eye and stop the djinn. If that *is* what you want?"

Luca walks over to meet Arabella by the wall. "It does make sense. But what if we're wrong?"

Arabella stays firm, she seems convinced this is the right thing to do. Luca is still unconvinced, however: "Are you sure? How do you know all of this?"

"My Dad. He taught me some stuff when I was younger and he was still around. Plus when I saw him the other week I may have asked him a few things about the djinn…"

Luca throws Arabella an annoyed look. Arabella smiles back innocently, causing Luca to finally relent.

"Fine. Let's just hope Moe doesn't ask about it ay?" He says, ripping the poster off from the wall, blue-tac and all. Once done, Luca turns to Arabella for approval. She nods reassuringly and rubs Luca's shoulder.

"Don't worry, there are some prayers we can recite to protect you. Let's make sure we're both up for Fajr prayer tomorrow morning and I'll show you."

The couple then take the poster outside, rips it to shreds and set it on fire. They link arms together and huddle close for warmth, while the shreds of paper melt into the ash of the fire pit. Luca and Arabella both breathe a heavy sigh of relief in the cold night air. Hopefully, this is the end of it.

* * *

Luca and Arabella finally get to sleep early the next morning. They got to bed about the same time that the birds began chirping, so the bedroom is fairly well lit. Arabella is led on her side, on the right of the bed in the fetal position; facing the window wall. Luca is led on his back, face up to the ceiling.

Everything seems normal, that is except for Luca's left hand, which is pointed upwards in the air. Two fingers outstretched and two curled in and down. He is unknowingly making a sign or symbol that esoterically means; "As above, so below".

Luca stirs, something in the room has changed and his body can sense the disturbance. He fidgets slightly in his sleep, moving sporadically as if someone or something were trying to wake him. Then Luca's eyes jolt open freakishly, but he is stuck rigid in the same position and can only just make out his surroundings.

Quickly, he notices something perched on the window sill to his right, looming over a sleeping Arabella. Luca slowly moves his eyeline to the direction of the intruder. As he adjusts his vision, it starts to become clear; the unmistakable shape and form of a djinn. This time it is curled and construed like a pretzel, rocking back and forth eerily.

Luca tries to talk but nothing comes out. Instead he can hear it as his own thoughts; fuzzy and unclear but quite noticeable. He tries again but no sound permeates from his lips. The thought however is louder and clearer. "What do you want?" asks Luca to the creature with his mind. The djinn instantly stops moving and looks straight over at Luca.

Its features aren't clear at first and obscured by shadow but its yellow teeth and blood red eyes sparkle like gems in the low light. Then it begins to come into focus and Luca soon recognises the curved horns, extending out from its brow like a wooden crown.

"You don't scare me; I've dealt with you before!" Luca thinks forcefully, his heart rate steadily increasing.

The djinn tilts its head curiously and grins, slime, and spittle from its mouth dripping onto Arabella's bed sheet.

"I said GO AWAY! GET OUT!" screams Luca internally, desperate now. The monster does not budge. Instead, it lowers one crooked claw down to the bed and runs a gnarly nail across Arabella's body.

"NO! You leave her alone!" Luca cries. After running its hand up to Arabella's hair, the djinn draws its hand back, licking the finger tips as if to simulate eating.

"You monster! Jesus Christ protects us. You hear me? The lord is our savior. He'll slay you down!"

The djinn snarls, meaning Luca's incessant praying is having some effect. Though unable to speak or move, Luca can sense the hesitation in the monsters movements and energy. Luca decides to up the ante: "Oh God, please let this work…"

He closes his eyes again and prays, harder and deeper than he has prayed in a long time.

"My Father, whom art in heaven…" Within moments the djinn has covered the area where its ears would be and screeches in pain. "…hallowed be your name. Your Kingdom come; your will be done…"

Now vibrating frantically, the djinn makes a high pitch frequency squeal before bursting into atoms and evaporating from the room. BOOM! Luca is startled out of his nightmare and wakes up in bed.

The room is empty, save for Arabella still sleeping peacefully next to him. Luca reaches under his arm and feels the sweat. He takes off his top and throws it on the bedroom floor. He looks back to Arabella and admires her sleeping, taking the time to calm himself down. He strokes her hair and tucks her quilt up tighter.

Looking at the window sill, Luca notices some scratches where the djinn was positioned in his dream. He squints at the markings closer; they do indeed look like they were made from some sort of sharp object. Luca shakes it off and tucks himself back into bed.

He will not be able to sleep now, however. Instead, Luca will just have to rest his eyes until Arabella wakes up.

"It is entirely possible that behind the perception of our senses, worlds are hidden of which we are UNAWARE."

Chapter 6

Attacked

It's the morning after the night before, and Arabella is sleeping alone in bed. She has moved from laying on her side, to her front. Luca on the other hand is nowhere to be seen. As the morning sunlight hits her rosy cheeks, Arabella stretches and yawns. In the background, she can just about make out the faint sound of a shower running.

It must be Luca she thinks to herself; up early and getting ready. After tossing and turning for a couple of minutes, Arabella finally admits defeat and gets up. Rubbing the sleep from her eyes, she sits up and looks around the room for a motive.

As she flicks off the covers, Arabella is startled by the beeping of a mobile phone. Her attention is drawn to Luca's work desk, where his phones rests, flashing. Arabella looks to the bedroom door; it is closed and the sound of running water still permeates through the walls.

Arabella debates with herself. Is it wrong of her to look? What if Luca returns too soon? Does she even want to know the answer to the worries which plague her? As she ponders, the phone goes off again. It is another message.

Arabella sees this as a sign and slides out of bed softly before tip-toeing over to the desk and swiping the phone. She opens the message and reads the text, her expression morphing from intrigued, to shocked, to sullen in a matter of moments.

In the shower, Luca looks up to ceiling and lets the cool water rinse off the remaining soap. Taking a large gulp of water from the shower head, Luca swills it around his mouth and spits the rest down the drain. Turning off the tap, he runs his hands through his scalp and opens the shower doors.

Stepping out, he grasps the towel from off the radiator and covers himself. After drying himself, he squares up to the mirror and examines his face. He looks slightly better than the last time he checked, despite the late night they had due to all the recent goings on.

His eye bags are receding and a good, natural colour is returning to his cheeks. Luca pulls a series of funny faces, smiles subtlety, and makes the sign of the cross. He leaves the bathroom and returns to his bedroom.

As he enters, he is greeted by Arabella; stony faced and back to the wall. Luca is oblivious at first and greets her as usual. "Buongiorno my dear!" he sings sweetly. Arabella stays silent. Luca proceeds to finish drying himself, unaware of her rising anger.

"I said, good morning…" Luca repeats, looking over to Arabella. Arabella frowns back at him and shakes her head. "Who's Becca?" Luca's face drops immediately. He goes to respond but Arabella cuts him off.

"That's two times now Luca. Two times too many." She

reveals his phone in her hand with the messages open from Becca. Luca goes a shade of pale white.

Luca: "Arabella, I… I don't know what to sa- "

Arabella: "DON'T!"

"But we didn't even sleep together."

"I don't care!"

Arabella chucks the phone at Luca in tears. He catches it but drops the towel in the process, leaving him standing naked in the middle of the room.

As Arabella grabs her things and leaves, she slams the bedroom door behind her; shaking the room. Luca examines his phone; he sees the messages from Becca and throws the mobile at his bedroom wall. "FUCK!" he yells, before face planting onto his bed.

* * *

The rest of the day and the immediate days that follow are a blur for Luca. Things only continue to spiral and Luca's true ability for self-destruction is unveiled for the first time. Just like a self-fulfilling prophecy. Luca picks up right where he left off the last time this happened, ignorantly attempting to dilute his guilt and pain with drink, drugs, and casual sex.

Nothing works and it really only succeeds in driving him down, deeper and further into despair. One Tuesday afternoon, Luca finds himself at a pub just outside of town. It is the third one on his crawl and he can't remember how he got here or when. All that matters right now is making the pain and the shame go away.

He sits alone, in a beer garden; nursing a pint of Guinness. It is fairly empty, despite the good weather, allowing Luca to sit and stare into space blankly. As he drinks and smokes and whiles away the day, a series of voices plague his mind.

Constantly reminding him of his faults and failings, driving him to edge of insanity as he tries to work out how he got himself into this predicament yet again. He slaps his head in anger repeatedly, begging for the berating to stop. It is no use:

Luca's voice: "You're one of the most beautiful girls I've ever seen."

Mischa's voice: "What, don't you like what you see?"

Arabella's voice: "Did you mean anything that you said?"

Luca's voice: "I'm sorry, it was a mistake!"

Becca's voice: "I would never treat you like that."

Khalid's voice: "I hope you're taking care of my daughter."

Luca's voice: "Please Bella, you're the best thing that ever happened to me!"

Mohammed's voice: "Sounds like djinn to me... like a genie but evil..."

Arabella's voice: "Solomon's ring, it could control demons and spirits."

Luca's voice: "Leave me alone! You can't harm me, God protects me!"

Arabella's voice: "Where did you get that poster, we should burn it."

Luca is so distracted that when another publican taps him on the shoulder, he jumps up and almost knocks over his drink.

"Oh God, I'm so sorry mate!"

Luca turns around and is greeted by the rowdy publican, who also appears to be pretty intoxicated. Luca quickly shakes of his shameful sins and puts on his "public mask". He reluctantly forces a smile for the man.

"You got a lighter I can borrow?" the stranger asks, holding up a cigarette for Luca to see.

Luca swiftly hands the man his lighter and takes another comforting sip of his drink. The man sparks his fag, returns the lighter to Luca and walks on. "Cheers mate!" he hollers as he leaves.

Once he has gone and out of sight, Luca turns back to his drink and buries his face in his hands. He brushes his hair back, revealing the tears welling in the corner of his eyes.

Wiping them away with his sleeve, Luca pulls out his mobile phone and searches for Mohammed's contact. Upon retrieving it, he calls the number and puts the phone to his ear. The phone rings for a few seconds before someone answers.

Luca: "Hello?"

There is no reply.

Luca repeats again: "Hello? Mo? You there?"

Still no answer. "HELLO!?"

The response makes the hairs on Luca's neck stand on end. A high pitched scream rattles though the speaker, followed by a series of inconceivable jargon in another language; demonic in sound. *"'Ahmaq, sawf 'aklu ruhik"*. Luca cancels the call straight away and slams his mobile on the beer garden bench. "Leave me the fuck alone!"

Luca is breathing heavily when he notices the man from earlier look over from the other side of the establishment. Luca promptly necks the rest of his Guinness drink and makes a quick exit.

* * *

The remainder of the academic year is a haze for Luca. His interest in girls and partying wanes, until the supposed friends start to fall away and eventually leave him. His attraction, and attractiveness to the opposite sex depletes and instead he decides to focus on his studies.

It's not an easy feat by any means but ultimately a good distraction from all the pain and suffering he has caused and is currently feeling. Alas Luca gets on with life and turns things around; staying up late, library on weekends, even additional projects for extra credit. Before long and it's time for Luca to return home.

Luca says goodbye to classmates and lecturers, packs his things and cleans out his room. Just in time for his dad Vince, to arrive in djinn with a van to collect him and his things.

After seeing his Father properly for the first time in a while, Luca gives him the biggest, longest hug, almost breaking down in the process. After catching up and loading the van, the two make their way back to the small country town near Bristol, that Luca is from.

Entering the motorway, Luca looks back one last time at his university and the accommodations behind him. He sighs silently while his dad natters on about this and that, clearly excited to be bringing his son home.

They arrive back home later that day to the warm welcome of Luca's mother, Donna. Luca wastes no time in jumping out the vehicle and running into his mum's arms. Nothing feels quite as safe as the embrace of one's own mother.

Vince starts bringing in the stuff while Luca catches up with Donna, and soon they are all sat around the dinner table; eating together.

They laugh and joke and reminisce, but every so often Luca seems to drift off and Donna will have to remind him to cheer up and get rid of that "vacant look". Hours pass. The dining table is eventually cleared and they sit, sipping black coffee and foraging almond biscuits. Before long though, everyone is spent and they all decide to call it a night and head off to bed.

Luca clambers up to his old childhood room and drags himself under the covers. He lays there, overwhelmed, and exhausted. As Luca tightens the quilt around him, the warmth soon sends him off into a deep sleep. A sleep it seems that he has needed since forever! If only it were that simple though. Luca may have tried to forget his recent past but his recent past has not forgotten him.

Time passes, Luca sleeps on. More time passes and Luca snores, now in a deep, deep sleep. Then, at around 3AM (on the tip of the Devil's hour), it all begins again. In typical fashion, it starts with Luca's breathing, then his perspiration and uncontrollable spasms. Finally, Luca's eyes burst open.

All Luca can see is blackness and the faint outline of the assorted furniture that decorates his bedroom. As he moves his eyes around the place, he spots the outline of a man from within the shadows.

He stops, dials in, and focuses. All the time, his breathing becoming increasingly strained. Then, from within the void; two yellow pupils protrude out and pierce directly into Luca. "No, no, not again…" Luca says to himself.

The creature steps slowly forward, savouring the sense of dread seeping from Luca's pheromones. "This, this isn't real.…" Luca thinks, trying to convince himself.

The djinn is unaffected however and continues its approach. "This is just a dream; this is just my imagination."

As the monster passes Luca's bedposts, it vibrates; moving and rearranging its atoms like a shapeshifter. It assumes the form of a witch; old, haggard, and dressed in torn black cloths. Then the djinn (as the witch) drops onto all fours and changes yet again into a big black dog, growling as its reaches Luca's bedside.

Unable to move or turn his head, Luca becomes increasingly distressed. When will this torment end? Was this always his affliction or did he bring this upon himself!

The only thing that seems to work in halting them is a sincere prayer or the mention of a truly holy name.

Luca feels shame for even daring to speak God's name. Especially after the way he has treated those closest to him recently. But he has no choice; it is the only thing he knows which works.

Luca looks out into the middle distance and mentally calls for help: "Lord God, I know I am not worthy…"

The djinn, now back in its original form and leaning over Luca's bed, claws at its own head and writhes around in pain.

Luca continues, trying to remain unfazed. "Please, forgive me for my crimes. Grant me penance from this eternal torment!"

With those final words and the intention behind it, the

djinn is startled and loses its power. It whines and wails as it is forced to retreat to whence it came.

At the same time Luca awakes fully from his night terror and springs into action. He stumbles out of bed, falls onto the carpet, and assesses the room whilst panting.

Luca looks down at his hands, reassuring himself of his return to reality. Then from somewhere in the bedroom, a creak catches his attention. Afraid, he jumps up and launches himself through his bedroom door and down the hallway.

Luca turns a corner and rushes through a door at the far side of the house. He ends up in his parents' room, who are both fast asleep in bed. Luca gets a feeling and stops in the doorway, chancing another look back... nothing is there.

Luca's Mum, Donna, wakes up first and rubs her eyes to see Luca stood in the doorway, silhouetted only by the hallway light. For a split second he resembles the shape and form of a djinn. Donna taps Luca's Dad, Vince, on the shoulder and wakes him also.

The two adjust their vision to Luca, as he steps forward into the room and switches on the bedroom light. His pupils are heavily dilated, sweat patches are dotted all over his shirt and he seems to be unnaturally drained of energy.

"What's wrong babs?" Donna asks wearily.

Luca says nothing, he just stands there trembling.

"Hey Luc, you OK?" adds Vince.

Luca just bursts into tears and runs over to the bed and hugs his parents passionately. The couple instinctively comfort Luca back but at the same time, look to each other in concern.

* * *

Not long after and Luca is sat with his Mum, Dad, and youngest sister Chiara. They are huddled together around the dinner table, consoling Luca over the night's events. The kettle clicks in the background, prompting Vince to make some drinks and bring them to everyone.

"Thanks Vince." Donna says, as she accepts her cup of tea. "Thank you." Mimics Chiara also. Luca just nods and smiles, still sniffling from his emotional outbreak earlier.

Vince: "Where's all this negative talk coming from Luca? I mean you're a good looking guy, you're young, just graduated from university; you really should be happy… proud even."

Donna shoots Vince a sarcastic glare as she sips from her mug. "I think that's fairly obvious Vince!" she retorts.

Vince looks at Donna and back to Luca. "Well explain please, 'cos I don't understand it!" he replies adamantly.

Luca sighs, building up the courage to be fully open and honest for once. He ponders a moment, before deciding to let it all spill out. He finally answers: "It's her; "Bella". I fucked it all up, big time! Now I can't help feeling like I'm damned because of it."

Donna screws her face a little and replies gently. "Aw hon, you think you're the first person to cheat, or go through heartbreak?"

"No, I know that." Luca quickly agrees. "It's just, despite any issues we may have had, she was always good to me. I mean, I had the rare opportunity of a lifelong relationship but I threw it all away… and for what, sex? I'm so stupid!"

Vince holds out a hand as if to give Luca a break and offers some keen advice. "OK, so you made a mistake. Big deal, who hasn't? If you are really meant to be together, you will find your way back. If not? Then it was never meant to be!"

"Yeah, she was a nice girl but she wasn't perfect either. You had to change, to compromise too much. So although you certainly acted out wrongly, your feelings were just. Everyone has faults! Besides, we do not want our son to change who he is, in anyway, for anyone, especially not for some girl."

Luca turns down his mouth. It is hard to hear the truth sometimes but deep down he knows they are totally right.

Vince leans in and looks directly into Luca eyes.

"Look, say you did change and become the perfect example of a man that *she*, or anyone, wants. Romantic, successful, dotes on her, converts, and agrees with all her morals and ideals. Cool. But then imagine twenty years from now. Imagine something else happens and it does not work out, for whatever reason. What then? You'll have compromised your very essence for a null result."

The usually quiet Chiara chimes in here: "Change should come from within, not from outside. Or else you're just covering up... not genuinely making a difference."

Vince, Donna and Luca are taken aback by Chiara's wise words and smile with pride. Donna puts her cup down and leans in too. "Luca, you gotta stop being so hard on yourself. The fact that it bothers you this much, shows that you care, shows that you're not an evil person!"

Luca seems a lot more relived now. He takes a sip of his own tea for the first time and ruminates on his families advice. He is so lucky to have them.

The whole family sit still in silence for a moment before Chiara piques up again. "So, what did it look like? I want details!"

"Huh?" Luca questions his little sister.

Chiara: "The djinn, what did it look like?"

Vince: "No, enough of that."

Donna: "Yeah, let's not encourage it please."

Luca is unoffended but ignores the question all the same. The truth is, he is not really sure. He can feel their energy and intentions more than get a clear picture; such is the nature of sleep paralysis.

"Thanks guys. You are so understanding. I do not know

what I would do without you. And I'm sorry again, for putting you all through this nonsense."

"You don't have to ever apologise to us about something like this. You're our son." explains Vince, honestly.

"Yeah, we'll always be here for you. Just stop keeping things bottled up. It's not good for you or your depression."

Luca lowers his head in acknowledgement. Chiara stands up and walks around the table. She reaches into her dressing gown pocket and pulls out a silver chain necklace. Attached to it is small round orb, light blue in colour. Luca looks up at his sister, surprised.

"It's an "Iblis Orb". Apparently it defends against spiritual attacks." She explains.

Luca smiles and mouths "thank you", clutching onto the necklace tightly. Chiara in turn, smiles back and leans in to cuddle him. "Wuv u Wuca!" she says playfully.

Donna and Vince also get up and join in the big family hug.

Donna: "Yes, we're always here you. Don't forget that."

Vince: "Ah come here silly!"

The four of them stand and comfort one another in silence as Luca cries tears of joy. He's finally taken off all of his masks and spoken his truth. For the first time in a long time.

In the coming weeks and months, Luca adjusts to life back at home. He graduates and gets his degree, renovates his bedroom, and starts applying for jobs. At the same time he resolves to find out more about his supernatural experiences and put an end to all this once and for all.

* * *

His journey of healing begins with a visit to a local witchcraft themed shop. Following the address on a business card, given to him by a family friend, Luca navigates his way around the backstreets of his home town. After taking a couple of twists and turns, he eventually finds the shop, nestled between a church and a hairdressers of all places.

It is called "Spell Cast" and even from the outside, emits a distinctly gothic and dark vibe. Carefully folding the business card and placing it back in his pocket, Luca checks his appearance in the window reflection and promptly enters the shop.

The bell jingles as Luca enters and he is greeted by two goth girls, who were chatting between themselves at the counter. "Hello!" says one of the assistants, turning to Luca. "Hi..." Luca replies, waving a hand. "How can we help?" asks the second girl.

"Um... I am here to see Tina? I have an appointment."

The first girl pulls out a binder from beneath the till. She opens it and flicks through to today's date. Scanning through the names, she finally comes across a time with Luca's name next to it. "Name please?" she asks.

"Uh, Luca. Luca DiMarco." He replies promptly.

"Yup, it's here." the goth girl acknowledges. "Just a moment, we'll see if she's free now."

The first girl nods to the second, who opens the plush, purple velvet curtains behind the counter and heads into the back. All the while, Luca looks on nervously.

"Take a seat if you like." the first goth girl offers, returning to her chores. Luca smiles appreciatively but instead decides to take a look around the store. He examines the products on offer; there's incense, candles, crystals, spell books and all other sorts of witchy paraphernalia.

One particular book catches Luca's attention. The cover depicts the "Hand of Fatima" or "Hamsa Hand", a symbol used to ward off evil eye and curses. A quick scan of the cover suggests that with this book, the reader can ward off: envy, jealousy, love rivals, competitors, negative spirits and even djinn. He opens the book and scans through, just as the second goth girl returns from the back room.

The second goth girl: "Tina's ready for you now. Wanna come through?"

"Yes, thanks!" Luca says, closing the book and returning it to its rightful place on the shelf. The store assistant gestures for Luca to follow her into the back. He obliges and she holds back the velvet purple curtain for him to enter. On the other side, in the backroom, a more mature lady sits in front of a small coffee table. On the table are a deck of tarot cards and a burning oil lamp.

The lady, a "witch" called Tina, stands up and greets Luca as he enters. Smiling sweetly to ease his tension.

Tina: "Hello, how are you?"

Luca: "I'm OK, thanks. I mean... I've been better, but it depends how this all goes I suppose. Haha."

They both share a laugh and sit down on opposite sides of the table. "Not to worry hon. What you must remember however, is that good and bad are both relative terms. What I am doing will only tell you the truth; the facts. How you interpret them though, is entirely up to you."

Luca clears his throat and tries to appear more serious.

"Sure, I understand. And just for the record, are you a good or bad "witch"?"

"Oh I'm most certainly a white witch. Or a good witch, for lack of a better term."

Luca seems visibly more relaxed, and Tina notices. She smiles to herself, and realises that this is going to be an interesting reading to say the least.

"Don't worry, I'm not going to put a spell on you!" Tina chuckles.

Luca gulps slightly, but it's too late to back out now.

With that, Tina picks up the tarot deck and starts to shuffle them. "Now I want you to relax." she states, continuing to shuffle. "Clear your mind of any and all unwanted thoughts. Find a centre and focus on that. What do you want to learn about yourself today?"

Luca nods accordingly and watches on as Tina finishes mixing the deck and places it face down back on the table.

"This is important." Tina continues. "Whatever it is you want. Hold on to that thought, that feeling, and do not stray... Otherwise it may corrupt the reading. Now, when you are happy, shuffle the deck." She pushes the tarot cards over to Luca and motions for him to proceed.

"OK, got it." asserts Luca, accepting the deck. He sits up in his chair, closes his eyes and starts to shuffle. While he mixes the cards up even more, he consciously pours into it all his thoughts, feelings, dreams, intentions, and emotions.

At the same time, Tina also closes her eyes and makes some obscure hand gestures that Luca is unfamiliar with. It would seem as though she is "centering her chi" or "balancing her chakras", in an attempt to connect to the spirit world.

Whilst she continues to meditate and focus the energy of

the room, Luca finishes with the cards and places them face down again on the table, sliding the deck back over to Tina.

Luca then waits patiently as she completes her process of "tuning in", and it's not long before the atmosphere in the room literally changes. Only ever so slightly at first but it's a change that is unmistakable to Luca now.

It is like the atoms in the air have become electrically charged, causing the candles to flicker and sway in the opposite direction. There are no windows or doors to the room, and no air current either but the flames dance and swirl all the same.

Then abruptly, they stop moving and return to their normal positions. Senses heightened, Luca's eye dart from the candles around the room and back to Tina again. Tina slowly opens her eyes and smiles at Luca, knowingly.

Tina: "Now, with that thought still at the forefront of your mind, split the deck in two."

Luca takes a deep breath and nods, appropriately cutting the pile in half. Then, Tina picks out seven cards from the middle and places them down on the table, turning them all face up in the process. She looks over the selection and orders them accordingly. Luca watches on intently, curiously excited about the whole process.

"Phew! OK." States Tina. "There's a lot of information here. This might take us a bit more than an hour."

Luca grins awkwardly, unsure if this a good or bad thing. "Well, I don't have any other plans today…" Luca jokes in return.

Tina smirks back. "Well, that's good then…. Right. So firstly, what this is telling me, is that you are really struggling right now. Mentally, financially, and romantically. You are all off balance and askew. In regard to finances especially, this should not be the case. But the decision is down to you really. It could get better *or* it could get worse… it all depends on the life paths you choose to take."

Luca leans in closer. Tina elaborates: "You're an intelligent guy, who in theory should be quite comfortable; affluent even. However as it stands, you are willingly choosing base indulgences and temporary pleasure over long term peace and prosperity. This may be due, in part, to past lives. I can sense that your soul has inhabited the vessels (or bodies) of many people, over many lifetimes and usually of higher social standing. You rarely wanted for much and were generally well looked after and respected."

Luca is trying to remain unbiased but something inside him knows what Tina is saying to be true. There is something undeniable about the strength of his intuition in this case.

In the moment, Luca thinks back to something he once read in his spiritual research. Often it is our gut instinct which informs us correctly first. Before we let our mind and emotions wander, confusing or skewing the initial message.

Tina: "This is not to say that you're being punished now. In fact, *you* chose to reincarnate yet again. To come back and experience this material plane one more time. It would seem you wish to experience a humbler life, to work a bit harder for your success, to centre your moral compass and round out your character more wholly through life lessons."

Luca is gob-smacked, although he tries not to show it. What she says rings true. How could she know these things. Is she truly psychic, a real witch? Luca himself has seen and heard stranger things. Regardless, he yearns to know more.

Luca stutters: "Do you know where I've been, who I was or what I've done before? In these past lives, I mean…"

Tina sits up in her seat and looks straight on at Luca. She almost goes cross eyed as she reads Luca's aura; the energetic field that surrounds and penetrates all living things. To a clairvoyant, the etheric waves appears as varying colours representing different moods and emotions.

Once Tina feels that she has gathered all the information she can, she elaborates.

"Well that's no easy feat. For starters, there were many lifetimes; making you an old soul. This is evident in your unexplained attachment to older music, fashion styles and morals. The strongest ones that are coming through to me, is your roles as the son of a chieftain in a Congolese tribe… as well as being a priest in one of the Egyptian courts. These past life experiences taught you strength, wisdom, leadership, and spiritual skills. All which are now helping you to fulfill your soul's purpose in this life! And although you were relatively affluent in these other timelines, you still had a generally good heart and honest nature. This has carried through with you to the present day, however you risk wasting this opportunity by turning your back on what you have learned. Are you following?"

Luca is pretty much in awe at this point, although he tries hard not to show it too much. "So far, so good." He assures Tina.

"Good." Tina agrees, continuing her reading. "The solution to your financial problems is restraint and a deeper understanding of the value of money. It is a tool, a means to and end and can build great things or equally, and just as easily, destroy. Although this sounds like common sense, this is not first nature to you, due to your mostly comfortable past experiences."

Tina gives Luca a moment to catch up, she understands this must be a lot of information to digest.

"On top of that, you have brilliant ideas *and* the appropriate gifts with which to manifest them. However, you are continually shutting yourself off from them. Your mind is... elsewhere, preoccupied... with a love, or an ex? Am I right?"

Luca nods, his eyes unable to not reveal his surprise. "How do you know all this?" he relents.

Tina giggles to herself and turns her hands up. "You're quite easy to read actually. You wear your heart on your sleeve. This is because you are especially sensitive, both internally and in regard to others. We call people like this "empathic"."

Luca takes a deep breath and shakes his head in acknowledgement. "Woah." he mutters simply.

"You must let her go. You two were not meant for each other, not in this current timeline anyway. It seems you were indeed lovers in a specific past life and have met multiple times, before and since. You share a karmic bond; a connection formed between souls, to help each other learn and grown when incarnated on Earth. This may be why you were so drawn to each other in the beginning and why deep down, you find it hard to give her up completely. You must realise that at its core, this relationship is toxic. Reason being, it was all a lesson about selflove *not* about loving others."

Luca looks emotional now, like he might cry at any moment. He tries to hold it all in but it's all too much. His eyes go red and glaze over as he sniffles quietly. Tina softens her tone appropriately, so as not too cause Luca too much distress but pushes on as he really needs to hear this revelation.

Tina: "Only when you let go completely, will you be able to find true peace. As of now, you have given up all your power to her. She controls you now, both mentally and emotionally. This is not only stopping you from moving on physically but stunting and stagnating your spiritual growth as well."

Luca wipes the tears from his eyes and laughs at himself to break the tension. "Flipping hell. Anything else? Haha…"

"Here." Tina hands Luca a box of tissues form the side. He takes a few and cleans up properly. "Thanks Tina." he replies, dabbing the remnants off his cheeks.

"When I asked you to shuffle the deck, you were visited by a guardian spirit. A male relative I believe, who has passed on to the other side. He wanted to contact you, to let you know he is watching over you; that he loves you and that you are blessed."

Luca perks up at this instantly and mutters under his breath: "Nonno?"

Tina turns down her lips and tilts her head to one side. "Possibly. He was accompanied by two other spirits, far more powerful; angels maybe. They advised him that it wasn't his place to intervene and escorted him away."

"Seriously!?" Luca balks.

Tina chuckles. "Yes, seriously. And we're not finished yet..."

"This is explaining so much to me, thank you, really!"

Tina waves her hand apathetically. "Oh, you'd be surprised. Listen, I am not a religious person; not by any means. Not in the classical way anyway. However I do understand its importance and value in society and human life. My own personal belief is that there is a "paradise" of sorts, a place where our spirits return to when our physical bodies die. A place where we can go to rest once we have completed our lessons and tests here on Earth. There is no such thing as hell though and certainly not in the classical sense. No fire and brimstone or lakes of lava. If anything, Earth is the closest thing to hell but is probably more accurately described as "limbo" or "purgatory". It's where we all come as souls to develop our universal knowledge and iron out spiritual flaws, before being inducted into the next stage of the school of life or returning to the source."

Luca exhales deeply shakes his head in wonderment. "And where do I fit on this scale?" he asks.

"Only you truly know the answer to that question. Having said that though, your soul is well lived and I would say you are pretty close now. What you must realise though, is that you *chose* to incarnate. Or at least agreed to it, all for the purpose of personal growth and development."

Sitting back in his chair, Luca takes another tissue from the tissue box and wipes his nose. "Phew, this is... a lot to take in! Haha."

"Very true! But it's what you do with this information next that is most important."

Luca puts his hand up instinctively. "I have a question..."

Tina: "Sure! You can put your hand down though. Hehe."

"Sorry, sorry." Stutters Luca. "Have you... have you heard of the "Djinn"."

Tina sighs, curiously. "I have come across the term before. They go by many different names and titles: djinn, genies, demons, spirits, ghosts. However they are not much different from us. They are born, they live, they grow, they die. They eat, pray, love, and reproduce even. Thought not all of them are evil or nasty, as you may have come to believe. Furthermore they're not the only other "supernatural" species to interact with us humans."

"The reason I ask is that I've had a lot of contact with them, especially over the last three or four years. Usually the visits are bad in nature, and I just wondered if you know of any ways to get rid of them?"

"Sure, it's a two factor approach. You must first purify your body and mind of inauthentic thoughts and actions. By that I mean thoughts of doubt or fear. Anything that can cause confusion or distraction with your inert being. In fact, any acts of self-destruction or wanton addiction will hinder you. Instead, find strength and honour in self love and care."

"OK... easier said than done though right?"

"It's all down to you my love. There are an infinite amount of paths and options laid out for you. But it's you who has the ultimate control over which route you eventually take. Hence free will."

Luca goes quiet for an extended moment, taking it all in. At the same time, Tina gets up and walks over to a nearby shelf. "I'm going to give you a number, it's for a friend of mine. Her name is Karen and she specializes in past life regression." Tina takes an address book off the shelf and sits back down opposite Luca.

"Maybe she can give you some more answers, advise on your next moves and help you decipher the patterns of your past." Tina opens the address book, finds Karen's details and writes in on the back of a "Spell Cast" business card.

"Tell her Tina recommended you." she advises, handing the card over to Luca. Luca smiles and nods, a subtle glow now illuminating his usually forlorn features.

Luca: "Thank you Tina, you've helped so much already."

Tina: "Don't worry about, it is my job after all. Haha. But please, if you take just one thing away from this whole thing, make it this: JUST DO SOMETHING! Move, travel, talk, dream, have fun, keep moving. Do not let your life come to a grinding halt for someone else. No matter how pretty. Whatever talent, passion, interest, or skill it is you possess; use it. Do not be hung up on the past and what could or should have been. Because clearly it was not meant to be. And that is OK. That is life. After all, everything happens for a reason. There are no coincidences, only signs and symbols. Even if we don't understand there rhyme or reason at the time…"

* * *

A few days later, and we find Luca stepping off a bus in an unfamiliar part of town. As the drone of the bus engine dissipates into the distance, Luca pulls his backpack tight over his shoulder and holds up a piece of paper with an address on it.

He mouths the street name and number to himself repeatedly as he looks around for the correct house. He soon realises he is on the wrong side of the road and crosses over appropriately.

After a short walk further down the street, he comes to the premises. He knocks on the door and after a brief wait, is greeted by a mature lady who welcomes and gestures him to come inside. "You must be Luca. I'm Karen, nice to meet you." Luca shakes her hand and nods.

Inside, Karen leads Luca to a conservatory at the back of her home. She pulls out an old leather recliner, not dissimilar to one found in a psychiatrist's office. She motions for Luca to take a seat, while she too gets comfortable herself. Once they are both relaxed, Karen takes out a pen and notepad and starts to write.

Karen: "Now I understand you went to Tina for a reading. And now you would like to find out more about your past lives, is that correct?"

Luca clears his throat. "Yes, that's correct."

"So what initially made you want to visit Tina for a reading?"

"It's a long story." Exclaims Luca.

Karen chuckles to herself. "Well, we do have time! Knock yourself out…"

Luca smiles and relents. "Well, from a young age I've always had this feeling that there's definitely more to this world than what I could just see and touch. I also used to have these very vivid dreams, which I didn't realise at first; but were actually predictions of things that would come to pass. That, combined with my Christian schooling, kept my mind open to the possibility of the supernatural."

Karen nods encouragingly as she continues to take notes.

Luca elaborates: "Anyways, things magnified when I started experiencing sleep paralysis and night terrors. These included visitations by what I can only describe as demon-like entities. I believe my interactions with these things, from a relatively young age is what contributed to me being diagnosed with depression and bipolar. I've tried to stay on top of it but in all honesty, it's made my life a secret misery ever since."

Karen looks up from her notes.

"And what about now? Are you still suffering?"

Luca seems nervous, he plays with his hands. "I haven't been visited in a while. Not since I've started making some changes in my life but I don't know how long it will last. They've come and gone before…"

Karen rubs her chin, curiously. "And what changes were they exactly?"

Luca adjusts himself in the chair comfortably. "Well moving away from London after I finished uni was a big one. Letting go of certain unhealthy relationships that were holding me back was another. I know I need to do more still, like living a healthier lifestyle and being more spiritual but I'm taking the right first steps, I believe."

Karen nods again and makes some more notes in her pad. "That's good, these are the essentials if you want to balance your mind, body and soul and open your chakras to experience higher states of consciousness. Then, the possibilities are endless. Like opening your third eye and developing clairvoyant abilities for example. How do you feel in yourself today?""

Luca shrugs: "Better than I have been in a long time. But I still feel like something's holding me back."

"Well, let's see if we can't do something about that." Karen says, putting her notepad and pen down momentarily.

"Now, I want you to close your eyes and take seven slow, deep breaths. Counting down from seven in your head."

Luca nods and adjusts the chair to a more horizontal position. He then closes his eyes shut tight and begins to pray.

"Now clear your mind and just let everything go, until you feel light as a feather."

Luca's breathing gets softer and quieter. His eyes relax from a wincing state to a peaceful one. Karen picks up her journaling materials and proceeds with the regression.

"I want you to imagine you're weightless, floating through the vast void of space. There are no sounds at all, apart from the sound of my voice. Karen's voice. Everything around you is black and cold but there are the twinkle of stars in the distance; shimmering like diamonds. You look down and see the Earth, as if you were an astronaut of the International Space Station. Watch the beautiful blue and green marble as it rotates on its axis. Take in its awe and majesty but also recognize the chaos and suffering that is needed to balance and support it. The cold, death, hunger, and violence. All the qualities of life we would rather forget but are just as important and necessary. Now once you have fully accepted those thoughts, go and reach out to your ancestors, your guides, and past selves. Ask them for help, ask them to show you the way!"

Luca appears to be sleeping now but in truth it is more like he is hypnotized. His consciousness has left his body and is travelling through the astral plane, on a journey to discover more about his past. "I... I feel it." Luca mumbles.

"What do you feel?" asks Karen.

"I feel... a connection."

"A connection to where?" she probes.

"To South America... no, it's Africa."

Karen writes that down in her pad. "OK, now following that feeling, let it take your hand and show you the way."

Luca's fidgets slightly in the chair: "It's taking me... I'm there, I'm there..."

As Luca repeats the words, he is drawn deeper into the dream state consciousness. Inside his mind's eye, Luca appears as a young Congolese boy in the midst of the African underbrush.

Adorned in a makeshift "nappy" made of straw and

leaves, he stands poised amongst the foliage. The boy's father is stood behind him, clutching a crude but sharpened spear. Ahead of the father and son, no more than ten to fifteen metres away, is a female lion unaware of their presence.

The father is teaching his son how to hunt. As he pulls back his arm to launch the spear, three lion cubs come skipping out of the shrubbery. The mother lion greets her babies with sniffs and a rub of the nose, before licking them each clean.

The father sighs and lowers his spear, causing the boy looks up at his father confused. The father explains that without a mother the cubs would not survive, and that this would upset the delicate balance of the ecosystem. They must wait to find an already ill or outcast animal, so as not to upset the circle of life. They can wait for a few more days if needs be.

Suddenly Luca is whisked away again, he cycles through time until he finds himself at a stream, deep within the jungle. He is the same boy as before but older now; maybe late teens or early twenties. He is skimming stones across the water, trying to get the attention of a young girl on the opposite side. The girl ignores the boy, pretending she does not see him.

Instead she is preoccupied with filling jugs of water; there are three full ones already neatly stacked behind her. The boy decides to switch up his technique and disappears into the jungle. The girl shrugs and continues her chores. Not one to easily be deterred, the boy sneaks around to the other side of the river and creeps up on the girl.

As she puts down the fourth jug, he sneakily attempts to push her into the water. Luckily, the girl manages to put her hands out in time, easing her fall. The boy laughs to himself and points mercilessly as she stands up in the stream, dumbfounded and dripping wet. The girl frowns and sputters, water spraying from her mouth in all directions.

The young man continues to belly laugh callously, and as he's distracted, the girl cups water in the palm of her hand and turns sharply, splashing it up into the boy's face. He freezes, shocked and admittedly, slightly impressed. The girl now laughs hysterically, while the boy stands grumpily on the shore.

After a moment, the boy raises his eyebrows and runs toward the water, jumping into the stream next to girl and drenching her from head to toe. The young adults don't hesitate in splashing each other aggressively, laughing and smiling all the more as they do.

The water fight then turns into a play fight, with the girl wrestling the boy into submission. Eventually, they both give up and back down, panting as they stare into each other's eyes lovingly. The boy leans forward, the girl leans forward too and they kiss passionately in the river under the beaming midday sun.

Just as Luca begins to really enjoy the experience, he is again ripped away from this moment and thrust further into this boy's future. Similarly he arrives in the body of the young adult; now a grown man, as he stands agitated around a campfire.

There are other tribesmen present around the flames too. They are all of different ages and social stature, stood with him in debate. They are arguing on the best course of action to take, in regard to a current problem within the village.

Whatever the issue is, they seem geared and prepped to fight; clutching various primitive weapons like spears and clubs in their hands. Behind them, most of the camp is in disarray.

Some tents are ripped or torn, while others are completely burnt to a crisp.

Frightened women and children are huddled under the shade of a large tree, wailing at the chaos around them. Our hero is tired of talking and grabs a small axe out of the dirt. He pushes through the crowd of men and charges into the jungle.

The other tribesmen start to holler and shout, also picking up their weapons and following behind him as they head to war. The villagers tear through the jungle like acrobats, jumping over rocks and logs, diving under branches and slashing through the thick undergrowth.

Eventually they come upon a group of fierce looking barbarians, outsiders of other communities who have come together to form their own illegitimate all-male tribe. The barbarians hear the villagers coming and rush to pick up their own weapons.

Luca watches on through the eyes of his man, as he pushes forward without hesitation, hacking down barbarians as he does. His people follow close behind, covering him from side attacks as he makes a beeline for his wife; the girl from the stream in the last vision. (Yes, they are married now but she has been kidnapped by these rapist, murderous outlaws.)

The man picks up a club from one of the fallen barbarians and attacks as many enemies as he can, akimbo. Eventually the villagers manage to overwhelm the barbarians and chase them out of their makeshift camp. Behind them they leave the bodies of some villager women that they have already had their way with.

One such woman, is the wife of our hero. He drops to his knees, covered in blood, and holds her limp, lifeless body. The small bump protruding from her belly reveals she was pregnant. More than six months by the look of it.

He looks up to sky and lets out a blood curdling scream which echoes through the forest. At the same time, the heavens open up and a torrential rain batters down on the jungle from above. Blood is washed away; fires are put out and the evil of the marauding tribe is purified that very night.

However some things cannot be mended and although our man returns home a hero to his tribe, to himself, he is no hero at all. He failed to do the one thing he promised to always do; protect his wife. No matter the cost.

As Luca's heart breaks in time with his ancestor, he is once again pulled out of the situation. A whirlwind of emotions bombard Luca as he is transported even further forward.

Opening his eyes, he finds himself on top of a cliff. The husband of the deceased wife is sat cross legged, mediating. He is an old man now, nearing the end of his life. Still heartbroken over the loss of the love of his life, he never remarried or sired children.

By his appearance, he has seen many battles and carries many scars. He also seems to be ill and looks especially malnourished. It seems as though he has come here to die peacefully, with the hope of being reunited with his sweetheart once again.

A tear rolls down the side of his face and falls off his chin. It is carried away by the strong breeze, which also brings to him a small Monarch butterfly. The butterfly lands on the old man's hand and stays there.

He looks down and smiles, he instantly recognizes it as the spirit of his dead wife. She has visited him to comfort him on his death bed and assure him that everything will be OK.

He lifts his hand up and admires the insect. The butterfly flaps it wings repeatedly, making a stunning pattern of colours. The old man leans down and rubs the butterfly with his nose, before standing up and releasing it again into the sky. The butterfly disappears into the horizon, whilst the man walks to the edge of the cliff and peers over the side.

He then looks up to the sky and prays in his own primitive, native language. Then without hesitation, he steps off the edge and plummets to his death. At the bottom of the ravine, his soul leaves his broken body and rises up into the sky, lifting higher and higher until it leaves earth all together.

The soul of the old man returns to the source, where it is greeted by an endless sea of other, conscious spirits. As he returns to his true home in the sky, the other entities part and allow the soul of his long lost wife; his twin flame, to come forward. The two long lost lovers embrace and dance together in joy once more.

There reunion is short lived however, as she confides in him that she has been called back down to earth. She still has more lessons to learn. He refuses to let her go but she has no choice in the matter. Soon he will have to return as well, for this is the way of things.

She tells him that the short time they had together was magical and that nothing magical lasts forever, for that is what makes it magical to begin with. She tells him to forgive, forget and let go of the past. For if it is meant to be, they will be brought together again.

And just like that, she is pulled away from her old lover and taken back down to the material realm once more. Luca stirs, he is gently coaxed back into the present by Karen who uses her voice as a guiding light. Eventually Luca manages to open his eyes again, which are admittedly heavy and strained.

He rubs them and slowly regains focus. Looking around the room, he sees Karen approaching with a cold glass of water. "Here, you'll need this." she whispers, passing him the drink.

Luca takes the glass and does not hesitate in downing the contents. "Thanks." he replies, putting the glass down and gasping for air. Karen returns to her own chair and picks her notepad and pen back up.

She quickly looks through what she has written down, tapping the pen on the pad a few times. She smiles at Luca and breaks the tension. "Well, well. That was quite something wasn't it." Luca nods and smiles back, still catching his breath. Karen continues. "So, what did you take away from that experience? What was the message you received?"

Luca looks around the room, deep in thought. He takes a moment, smiles to himself and answers. "That I need to let go."

"Interesting." Karen replies. "Let go of what exactly?"

Luca: "Of anything from the past. Anything that is holding me back. My ex. My mistakes. My shame, guilt, anger, sadness. All of it."

Karen nods and writes something down. "And what exactly do you feel you're being held back from?"

"From moving on with my life. From doing great things. From being the best version of myself that I can possibly be."

"And how does all that make you feel? Being held back from you dreams and aspirations?"

Luca sits up in the chair and makes himself comfortable. "I feel like subconsciously, deep down, I knew this answer all along. Coming here, doing this; just confirmed it all for me."

Karen sits up in her seat and leans forward slightly. "Good, that's really good. There is one more thing though…"

"Luca leans forward also. "Yes and what's that?"

Karen pauses for effect and then explains. "Forgiveness. Forgive yourself for your mistakes, for whatever sins you think you may have committed; learn from them and move on. Likewise, forgive those that you feel have let you down. Whether it is your ex, your friends, or the larger world in general. Forgiveness and love is the key. Forgiveness and love is the way. Forgiveness and love will set you free."

Luca is stunned by Karen's words; they really touch his soul and he knows now for sure that he is on the right track. He sits back in his chair and relaxes, taking in everything Karen said and everything else that he just experienced. He looks out of the window into Karen's garden and smiles, truly content and optimistic about the future.

* * *

That same evening, Luca rushes home with urgency. He is dedicated to figuring out this curse once and for all. He storms upstairs to his room and throws his work bag on the bed. Immediately he sits down at his desk, which is jam packed with books, DVDs and scraps of noted-paper scattered around.

All of them are on the same topic: The Djinn. Luca opens up one of his own journals and starts writing. He copies all the information from his laptop that he deems relevant. Basically, anything pertaining to the djinn and how to overcome them.

While writing and researching, Luca learns that the djinn, or djinni (plural), are always present albeit in a different dimension to ours. They can and do cross over from time to time, making themselves visible only to those they choose. Or indeed those already with the spiritual acumen to see the djinn freely.

For them to cross over however, they must use up a lot of energy. This energy they usually replace by feeding off of humans and other living creatures. The energy, called "loosh", they harness through emotions; primarily fear, sadness and torment. There are good djinn though, as well as the bad ones and some are even religious too!

The djinn are ethereal in nature, made of smoke and fire. They can, however, give themselves the illusion of a physical, material clay form like humans. They can also shapeshift, or appear to shapeshift, by telepathically altering their victims state of mind. Just one of the many telepathic powers they possess.

There are four main classes of djinn commonly recorded. They are the "Shayatin" (horned, devil looking), the "Ghul" (misshapen, fetus looking), the "Ifrit" (tall, clawed and bony) and the "Marid" (feminine, fiery and illusive). Luca works out that he has been visited by almost all types of djinn during his time suffering with sleep paralysis.

A preferred form for the djinn to take is that of a cat, black dog, snake, or bat. The six pointed star, also known as the "Seal of Solomon" is the best sigil to defend against a djinn attack. This is because of their intwined history with old King of Israel, who had special control over the djinn through the use of a magical ring bestowed upon him by God.

Another defense is the "Hamsa Hand" ("Hamsa" meaning "five") or "Hand of Fatima". This is because the djinn's prime motivation is jealousy or envy. They dislike the unlimited free will to create (and equal power to destroy) that humans have been given over earth and the material realm.

While they themselves are banished to the 4th dimension, an intermediary plane that is not totally physical or spiritual. More like a "dead zone".

Amongst all these notes are multiple drawings and sketches. They depict Luca's visions of djinn, other recorded accounts of sleep paralysis experiences and potential tattoo designs. The tattoos in particular, appear to be a branding of sort that Luca wants to use as protection.

Luca even goes so far as to trace the Congolese tribe that he had seen in his past-life regression with Karen. They are called the "Soukri", which means "to be thankful" and Luca agrees it's a fitting title, considering his experience of them.

After hours of research, Luca decides to call it a night and packs up his books and notepads. Upon doing so, Luca accidently uncovers an old photo of himself with Arabella from back at university. They both appear happy, beautiful and in love. A million miles away from how things did eventually turn out.

Luca mutters to himself "Shame." and returns the photograph to the notepad it fell out of.

He then finishes clearing up and gets into bed. He lays on his back and looks up to the ceiling. He smiles as he reminisces about Arabella and the good times of their relationship. He then takes his phone from his bedside table and opens up the old messages between them.

The last messages in the chat are Luca begging Arabella for a second chance, followed by her simple and straightforward reply: "I've met someone." He contemplates for a second, then deletes the chat as well as her number from his phone.

* * *

Over the next few weeks, Luca attempts to turn his life around. He takes to aerobic exercise and then running, waking up early each day to work out. Like a domino effect, this also leads to him starting a better diet of healthy foods and drinks.

He starts by cutting down, and then eventually eliminating meat from his meals. He also makes an effort to drink more water and ditches sugar, and other processed foods from his life. In a matter of days he is already seeing and feeling the results.

This gives him even more of a boost to continue on this path. Within a couple of weeks, he has been to a number of interviews and even accepted a new job at a construction firm designing logistical storage. Not exactly what he wants to do with his life but a step in the right direction, and a foot on the ladder.

In time, he even manages to squeeze in a date with a nice girl. It does not go any further than that but it was good in opening Luca up to the idea of relationships again. Eventually he finally saves up enough money for a tattoo and gets the designs he drew in his notebook, tattooed on his body.

The tattoos tells the story of Luca's spiritual struggle so far, albeit with a little embellishment for good measure. Luca even makes a few new friends at work and is invited on a night out with them. He is reluctant at first but eventually agrees to tag along, if only to bond with his colleagues more.

After a great night out, everybody starts leaving for home at around 1AM. That is except for Luca and his closest workmate Reese. The two wanna-be "Casanovas" come stumbling out of a bar together.

They seem merry but not completely blind drunk and in a generally good mood. As they walk down the high street, they pass a group of girls who giggle and smile at them.

The boys slow down and banter with them a little, before eventually moving on. Further on down the high street, they come across a homeless man who they stop and chat to for a minute. They give him some change and then carry onwards.

A fight also breaks out between two groups of revelers across the street but the boys just watch from afar. Before long though, the police arrive and break it up, leaving Luca and Reese to press on. As they continue, they pass a particularly nasty looking alley on the way.

Hanging about inside are a group of delinquents and destitute. They are huddled around in a circle together, probably doing drugs. One of the people in the group looks up from whatever they are doing and catches Luca staring. The man's eyes are dark and formless.

Luca meets his gaze for an awkward moment and the "druggies" eyes flicker from human to djinn in the flash of a second and back again. Luca shudders and swiftly turns away, catching up with Reese. "Hold up mate." says Reese unexpectedly. "I wanna get some more ciggies…"

Luca raises his half empty bottle of beer suggestively. "Cool, I'll wait here."

"Sweet. Won't be long." Reese replies, entering the off-license.

"Get us some "chewies" as well, will yah?" Luca adds.

Reese continues into the shop but calls back: "Got yah bro!"

Luca perches on a small wall outside the shop and sips his beer, watching the night life go by. As he finishes off the bottle and throws it into the bin outside the shop, a scantily clad woman walks past and eyes him up. She smiles and winks at Luca, gesturing to his genitals. Luca looks away but the woman, probably a prostitute, comes closer.

"Hey baby, do-" She says in a seductive voice.

"I'm not interested." Luca interrupts.

The woman puckers her lips up and puts a hand on Luca's shoulder. "Come on baby, don't be boring…"

Luca takes her hand and moves it away firmly. "I said no, get lost."

The woman kisses her teeth, offended. "Fine, fucking wasteman!"

The woman blinks and her eyes morph into that of a djinn. Her pupils appearing like black slits and the rest a vibrant, blood red. The woman flashes one last malevolent grin and struts away from Luca.

Luca is startled but unsure of everything anyway, now due to his current condition. As he stands there, slightly shook; Reese exits the shop and slaps him on the shoulder.

Reese: "Sorted mate!"

Luca jumps a little inside but hastily shakes it off and accepts the condiment. "Cheers bro…"

Reese unwraps his cigarette packet and pulls out a fag, lighting it. He offers Luca one but Luca declines. Reese shrugs and they both carry on down the road. Unbeknown to them however, someone or something is watching them and has its eye on Luca. It is a djinn. Invisible to any human but none the less, still powerful.

It is not uncommon for djinn to frequent the dirtier, darker parts of human society. This way they can prey of the weak-minded and sinful with relative ease. Tonight this particular djinn has its eye on Luca, and due to his drunk state and already weak mind, he will be an easy target.

Reese is pulling on his smoke and Luca is unwrapping his chewing gum packet, when the djinn leaves its hiding place and rushes Luca, knocking the wind out of him for a second. Luca wobbles from the impact and almost trips on his feet but is luckily steadied by Reese. "Shit! You alright mate?" he asks jokingly.

Luca sways on the spot, before managing to centre himself again. "Phew, yeah. Uh, that was close." He answers, bewildered at what just happened. Reese assesses Luca to make sure he's OK. "Ah you're fine. Your eyes are bloody red though haha! Been smoking a little reefer?"

Luca just looks confused. "No…"

Reese laughs and shakes his head, motioning for Luca to come. "Let's go man, otherwise we'll never get home."

Luca nods and follows Reese onwards. Sitting on the curb not a few metres away are two girls and a guy, innocently eating take way food and pizza. As the boys pass, Luca strangely goes over to one of the girls, unannounced. Completely out of character, he stands over her dominantly and demands her food.

The girl kindly refuses and out of nowhere, he leans down and snatches the box out of her hand. "Oi, what the fuck are you doing?" she yells. Luca gives her a dirty look, takes one bite of the pizza, and then throws the rest on the floor.

"You idiot! What a waste!" the girls adds, standing up to face Luca. Before anything can happen though, the boy of the group gets up and stands between the girl and Luca. He squares up to Luca, ready to fight. Reese, who *was* stood back laughing, now comes rushing over.

Everyone is shouting and the situation is escalating rapidly. Reese tells Luca to leave it but it is already gone too far. The boy motions to hit Luca. But Luca has already anticipated it and moves first, uppercutting the boy's jaw and sending him flying back. The girls immediately scream and start throwing things at him in defense. Reese grabs Luca and pulls him quickly. "Come on, let's go! There's "feds" everywhere!"

Just like that, Luca snaps out of his rage and comes crashing back down to earth. What the hell just happened? That was not like him at all. Luca looks around and sees a police officer approaching. "Run, now!" shouts Reese.

Luca turns away and runs as fast as he can, without looking back. The police officer who saw the altercation is in hot pursuit. Luca makes it about hundred feet away, when a bystander sticks out their foot and trips Luca. He drops to the floor and rolls, before managing to make it up again and continuing to run.

It's too late though, he has already lost too much time and the police officer has almost caught up with him. On top of that, two other officers approach from different directions and trap Luca in a pincer move. The officers tackle him to the ground and pepper spray him in the face.

Eyes streaming, Luca franticly tries to look around for help as the officers pile on top and restrain him. From across the road, Luca can hear Reese calling out for him. "Mate, are you OK? Don't worry, I'll come find you!"

Suddenly, a police van pulls up out of nowhere and Luca is bundled away.

* * *

Luca is awoken by a metallic knock, swiftly followed by a sliding sound, which reverberates around the cell. The "letter box" on the door opens and a stream of fluorescent light from the hallway cuts through the room. A pair of unknown eyes peer through the slit on the door and over at Luca; just in time to see him wake from his slumber.

The officer then passes a cup through the gap and onto the tray on the other side. "Water." the stern voice states. Luca pulls himself up on the concrete "bed" and looks over to the door. Before he can say anything, the officer is gone as quickly as he came.

Luca is still intoxicated, bloody and bruised from his arrest. He looks around the dark, damp, and cold prison cell. Markings from other ex-inmates scrawl the walls; tallies, names, threats… you name it. Luca huffs and shakes his head. How in the hell did he end up here? He thought he was on the right track! Sometimes it seems like things will never change; like *he* will never change.

Suddenly a sharp pain shoots up Luca's spine and into his head. Luca groans in pain and drops his head between his legs. He coughs and sputters, spitting blood across the concrete floor. Luca reaches two fingers down his throat and immediately brings up the contents of his stomach. He rushes over to the steel toilet in the corner of the room and vomits aggressively.

Wrenching, he makes sure it's all out, before proceeding to splash water on his face from the shoddy sink next to him. Whilst the water runs down his face, he takes a long, hard look at his reflection in the steely surface of the wash basin.

As he looks closer, he notices his eyes are bright red and his pupils slit like a snake or reptile. He jumps back in horror, tripping and falling onto the hard floor surface behind.

As he crawls back away from the sink, his hand falls on something hard and boney. He stops and lifts his hand, slowly turning to see the foot of a creature step back into the shadow of the corner of the room. Luca trembles.

He gulps and looks up, as two big yellow eyes flash open in the darkness. Shocked and confused, Luca musters all the courage he has and jumps up. He runs back to the bed on the other side of the cell and braces for anything.

Low rumbling sounds echo out from the far side of the cell, as Luca looks around for some protection but there is nothing to hand. Instead he clenches his fists and raises them ready to fight! As he does, the djinn appears out of the blackness.

It steps slowly at first, one foot at a time. Then it raises its right leg and appears to step on air. It rises higher and higher, until it's floating five-feet off the ground and gliding towards Luca.

Luca looks up in pure horror as it emanates above him, arms outstretched. Luca closes his eyes and clasps his hands together in desperate prayer.: "O dio mio, aituami, aiutami!" (Oh God, help me, help me!)

The djinn pauses mid-air about two metres away from Luca, who is now also frozen on the spot. The two "cellmates" stare at each other inquisitively. Luca gulps and slowly raises his left hand. As he does this, the djinn raises *its* right hand;

perfectly mimicking Luca's actions. It is as if they are a mirror image of one another.

So Luca raises his right hand as well and just like before, the djinn mimics the movement by raising its left as well. In this moment, Luca has another "awakening". These events and entities are causally linked to his own dark desires and shadow self. If he is to defeat this affliction, this curse, he is going to need to defeat a part of himself!

Then without warning the djinn flies forward again, jaws wide and elongated, arms flailing and slashing like knives. Luca lets out a blood curdling scream. As the djinn shoots right through Luca's body and stuns him momentarily. "Aaaaaaaaaaaagh!" he screams as the force of the attack sends him flying into the cold, concrete, cell wall

And then Luca wakes up, still in the cell but led back on the bed. He is sweating, ruffled and clearly distressed but otherwise OK. And there's certainly no sign of any djinn, despite the shouting and banging of other prisoners telling him to shut up. Luca sighs; another nightmare…

"The more fearful a person is, the more he uses his mind, The more fearless a person is, the more he uses his heart."

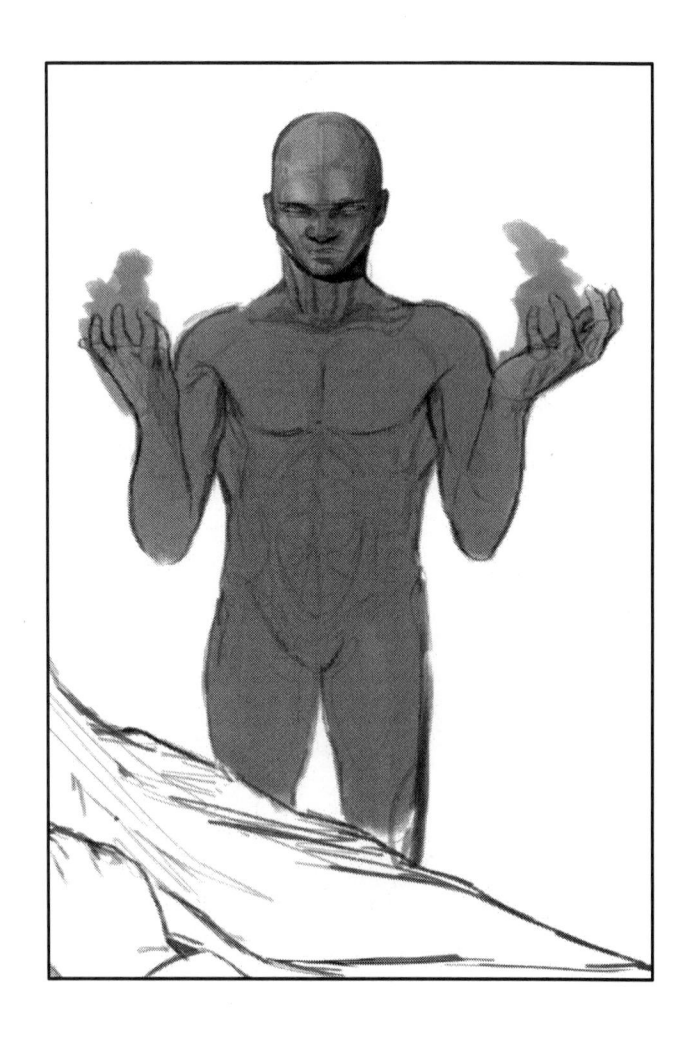

ACCURSED

Chapter 7

Accused

It's the day after the night before and Luca arrives at his family home barefoot, beaten and barley awake. He stops on the footpath, just outside the houses brick-paving driveway. Looking down at his cracked phone screen, he scrolls through a list of notifications; mostly from Reece. Luca shakes his head disapprovingly and puts his phone away again.

Instead he looks up to the sky. It's one of those dreamy, picturesque type of days, where everything radiates with a certain energy, an energy that invites the chance for change, an energy with a little extra "Je ne sais qua?" That is, everything except for Luca himself.

His clothes are ragged and stained, his hair is messy and unbrushed and his beard uncharacteristically overgrown, haggard and unkept. He truly is a sight to behold, standing out like a sore thumb amongst his quaint suburban surroundings.

Luca finds himself again in a familiar position; a common theme in his story it seems. But this time might honestly feel just a little different. This time feels like this is "it". Or close to "it" anyway. Luca looks up to the sky and closes his eyes, letting the sun soak into his skin. He makes the sign of the cross against his profile and finishes by bringing his hands together in prayer. He mumbles to himself:

"Oh God… Allah, Jehovah, Creator, Universe; whatever you are! I come to you humbled, hurt and heartbroken. I am not worthy of your love, help or grace. Yet I must ask you one last time. Please, show me a sign. Help me, save me and I'm yours…"

The very next weekend, Luca decides to visit his sister Tatianna in London. She is currently there studying psychology, and for Luca, it seems like a good way to catch up and get away from it all.

Whilst on the train, Luca reminisces on the times when he used to travel back and forth himself for uni. Sometimes alone, sometimes with friends, once or twice with Arabella too. He puts his headphones in (as is his preferred way to travel) and turns the volume up, gazing out to the rolling hills of the Cotswold's countryside; as the train shuttles on towards its destination.

While he listens on to his handpicked playlist, Luca unzips his bag and pulls out a fresh notepad. He opens it up and immediately starts journaling. He writes about how long it has been since his last "djinn incident", as well as his general mood, emotions and whatever else he has been up to or is lingering on his mind.

He finishes this current entry with a quote he heard once, a quote that he had almost forgotten yet suddenly seems suitably appropriate: "The journey of a thousand miles starts with just one step."

* * *

Later that evening and Luca arrives at Tatianna's house. He knocks firmly on the old, town house door and steps back, composing himself. After a few seconds, a blurry figure appears behind the frosted glass. After messing with the locks, Tatianna opens the stiff door with some force and immediately throws her arms wide to greet Luca. "Looca, hey!" she welcomes.

"Anna, hey!" he mimics back.

Tatianna steps to one side and gestures for Luca to enter. He shuffles past awkwardly with his travel bag in tow, setting it down at the bottom of the stairwell.

Tatianna closes the door behind them, locks it and turns to her brother again. She looks him up and down inquisitively.

"Aw, handsome boy... You've put on weight. You look good though!"

She attempts to pick his bag up but scoffs at the heaviness and puts it straight back down. Luca laughs, grabs the bag from behind Tatianna and follows her up the stairs. "Oh, and for the love of God, don't shave that beard. It really suits you."

Luca nods his head in agreement and makes a mock military salute. "YES SIR!" He jokes.

They both enter the kitchen together, it's the typical student accommodation; messy but functional. Luca finishes taking in his environment and puts his bag down on the kitchen island. Tatianna in turn heads over to the stove, where she's in the process of cooking an authentic Italian pasta dish. An assortment of ingredients are dotted on the worktops around her; garlic, onion, salt, and pepper, etc.

Luca sniffs the air greedily. "Mm, Pasta Fagioli?"

"Yep, and I hope you're hungry." Tatianna replies.

"Always!"

"Haha, good. Take a seat then."

"No, let me help." refuses Luca.

"It's OK, I'm pretty much done now. Just waiting for the pasta to be "El Dente", you know."

"Ah of course. Just like Nonno used to make it, eh?" Luca jests, throwing up his hands.

They both chuckle in unison at Luca's admirable impression.

Tatianna continues to stir the pasta in the pot. "So, how you feeling these days? How's the bipolar?"

Luca blows a raspberry and tries to think. He's taken aback but appreciates Tatianna's candor.

"Non ce' male." (Not so bad) he shrugs. "But a lot better than I have been in a long while."

"Hmm, what's up?" encourages Tatianna.

"...I don't know, I just feel a bit lost still."

"You still love her, don't you?"

"Well in a way, yes. I mean, I'll always care about her." Luca admits.

"You're definitely not over her." confirms Tatianna, returning to check the pasta.

"Yes, I mean no. Well maybe... but I know we shouldn't be together again."

Tatianna fishes out a single shell of pasta with a fork and flings it against the walk. It sticks!

"Not the same thing." She says, carrying on. "You need to forget about her, now. Get back into your writing, take up a new sport, anything!"

"I... I just don't feel passionate about those things anymore."

Tatianna turns the temperature down on the stove and puts the lid on the saucepan.

"Well whatever it is, you just need something to focus your time and energy into, something productive. That's the only way you're gonna heal."

"I know, you're right." Luca relents, sighing to himself.

"And Mum told me you got into a fight, or something. What's that about?"

Luca lifts up his hand and shows Tatianna the bruises on his knuckles.

"Ouch." she winces. "That's not like you!"

Luca suddenly looks uncomfortable. "Thing is, I don't even remember it. Just everything immediately before and after. It was like... one minute I was uptown having fun, and the next I was in the cells, banged up."

"You had a blackout?" Tatianna suggests.

"Maybe." Luca replies sheepishly.

"What about all this djinn stuff then? Anything there?"

Tatianna turns off the gas and readies the drainer.

Luca taps nervously on the wooden side of the kitchen island and looks out to the middle distance, biting his lip. "Nothing recently." Tatianna shrugs in response and pours the contents of the saucer, into the drainer, over the sink. Luca decides to change the subject. "So, anyways, enough about me. What's up with you? What's "the plan"?"

"The plan is… to have a good time and catch up with your lovely, beautiful, funny and exceptional sis!?"

"Haha. Sounds good to me."

"Don't worry bro, we'll have you over her in no time."

Tatianna winks at her bother as she starts to plate up the food. Luca smiles on, genuinely content, if only for a moment.

* * *

For the rest of the weekend Luca, Tatianna and her friends make the most of Notting Hill carnival. They dance, drink, and smoke the nights away, taking in all the vibrant sights and sounds of the big city at night. They also go to the cinema, just Luca and Tatianna, and enjoy the latest "Star Wars" film together.

Before they know it however, Monday morning has already come around and after a fun-filled few days, it's time for Luca to leave. Though it seems bittersweet, Luca has had the vital, positive, energy-boost he needed and has bonded even closer with his sister in the process. Life is funny, Luca thinks to himself. Even in the darkest of times, there's always still a silver lining. You just have to be open to finding it and receiving it.

* * *

That same Monday afternoon, Luca is stood outside the front porch of a hotel, waiting for his train back home to arrive. He is smoking a final joint and scrolling through his phone, headphones in and sunglasses on. He is bobbing his head in sync to the music, whilst intermittently taking more tokes of the spliff. After taking the final drags, Luca disposes of the roach-end by flicking it into a nearby bush and then takes out a fresh stick of chewing gum.

He takes no time in gnawing away at the stick of candy, relishing the much needed hydration on this hot summer's day. Adjusting his glasses, Luca looks up at the sun peeking it's comforting rays around the corner of a tall tower block, lighting up his face.

At the very same time, an Indian man (mid to late 30s) wearing a turban, walks past Luca on the pavement outside the hotel. The man, who judging his clothes, beads and turban, appears to be a "Yogi" of some sort, looks up just in time to witness this magical and rare moment.

In a split second, the sun's rays reveal Luca's aura in its entirety to the Yoga. The Yogi stares in awe, as Luca is illuminated by a bright white light and his true self is unveiled. The Yogi slows down as he passes Luca, before stopping and turning back around. He speaks in a broken English. "Sir, sir. I am so sorry."

Luca removes his headphones and smiles at the Yogi. "Yes?"

"Can I just say, you have the most blessed face, sir."

Luca looks around, both pleasantly surprised at the compliment but equally as concerned and confused.

He finally settles on a reply: "Wow, uh… thank you?!"

"Um, there is something else…" the Yogi continues.

"Yes?" replies Luca.

"God. God wants me to tell you something."

Luca scoffs, skeptical now. "Oh yeah, and what's that?" he relents, agreeing to humour the man for his politeness.

The yogi clears his throat before speaking again.

"God wants me to say that you are loved... and not to worry so much about silly things... everything will get better. Give it time."

Luca is taken a back. He drops his travel bag immediately and shifts his stance. He decides to play coy and tests the man.

"Well thanks. But I know that my friend. The question is, how do you?"

Luca firms up defensively but keeps a receptive smile on his face.

"I was told. Just now when I walked past you. I felt... I feel a connection and was given this message to say to you. I am just a messenger."

Luca folds his arms and leans in, more interested now.

"OK. Tell me more..."

"Do you have time?" the Yogi says.

Luca checks his watch and looks around the square anxiously.

"Well I have one hour until my train. So I gue-"

"That's perfect, plenty of time." interrupts the Yogi, taking Luca's hand. "The park, over there!"

The two men arrive at an unused bench in the middle of the small park, just across from the hotel. As they get comfortable, a couple of runners jog past them. Luca jumps instinctively and looks to the Yogi, slightly embarrassed.

The Yogi doesn't notice however and continues to make himself relax himself. Luca laughs it off and breathes in deeply, wiping the sweat from his palms on his knees.

Then the yogi strokes his beard and closes his eyes, muttering a short, inaudible prayer under his breath. Luca looks around uncomfortably but there's no one to see them, as luckily it's quiet in the park today.

Finally, the Yogi finishes and turns to Luca, opening his eyes wide. Yogi: "I am like a doctor you see, a doctor for people with sick souls."

Luca: "Like a Shaman you mean?"

"No, that is quite different. All you need to know, is that I am here to help you."

"Oh, thank you. Thanks so much."

"It's OK, no problems. Now let me tell you… your Grandfather. He loved you very much. When you were a baby, he blessed you, you see."

Luca's eyes widen underneath his sunglasses. The Yogi continues. "When you were born, he picked you up and kissed you. When he did, he blessed you. But no blessing comes without a sacrifice. For there is a balance to this universe and it cannot be upset."

Luca is stunned. How could this man know these details! He had only talked about this with his parents.

"More so, you have a nickname correct? Same as your Grandfather's?"

"Yes, well… kind of." Luca responds.

"Shining face. Am I right?"

"Faccia Lisca. It means "Smooth Face" in Italian."

The Yogi smiles and nods.

"Well, this means you two have an inert connection, deeper than the usual family bond. You share souls. When one suffers, so does the other. When one is "anointed", so is the other. But together you can break this wheel, this cycle; this… Karma."

Luca is moved to tears by the memory of his Nonno Pietro and all the information coming to light. It's as if deep down, he has known all of this all along.

"But you needn't worry, he is watching over you. He is trying to help you and guide you. So you can make the right choices now. To break the pattern. You see?"

Luca wipes the water from the corners of his eyes and smiles unabashedly. Granted he is crying tears of joy, but it's emotional all the same. He's just so thankful for this moment as this could be exactly the revelation he's been longing for. Luca unconsciously crosses his fingers in anticipation and takes another deep, calming breath.

Reciprocally, the Yogi adjusts himself to face Luca more. He holds Luca's hand and speaks clearly.

"You are having trouble with an ex-girl, correct?"

Luca goes pale slightly. He gulps. "Yes?"

"She has cursed you my friend. You know what the "evil eye" is?"

Luca raises his right palm and spreads his thumb and small finger slightly. "The hand of Fatima protects."

"Correct sir. So, because you cheated on this girl, she has cursed you not to find happiness. Now you have a difficult life. This was prophesied you see. Brought on to you by your Grandfather, for also doing such things. Now you must clear up this mess. It is up to you now, to break the curse."

Luca suddenly thinks of something. He jumps slightly in his seat.

"The Djinn!?"

"That is one of their many names, yes. They can be confused with "demons" or "bad spirits". Listen, you must be aware... because you are empathic, meaning your third eye is open, you are more attractive to these things. They can see you more clearly from their world, on the other side"

Luca begins to rub his hands nervously. "And what about now?"

The Yogi sighs and adjusts composure. "You have two attached to you right now, like parasites. And I can sense others sniffing around as well."

"TWO!" Luca exclaims.

The Yogi nods his head regrettably.

"Yes. One is from a previous life; you and your partner there had a baby but there was a tragedy, and the baby died. The trauma from this event caused the bad energy from its spirit to appear and attach itself to you. Through many generations and lifetimes."

Luca ruffles his hair; it is so much to digest. The Yogi rests one hand on Luca's back reassuringly.

Luca is shocked. He knew it was real all long but it's still just as sickening to hear it aloud right now.

"And the other one?" Luca asks the Yogi.

"The other one is a direct curse from your ex-lover. The one I mentioned earlier. It is with you because of a hex, a voodoo. It is tormenting you as a "job" if you will. Tell me, did this girl cut your hair?"

Luca's mouth drops slightly. "Yes! I used to have long hair, almost past my shoulders but she cut it for me one time. Made quite the mess of it actually, and I had to shave it off. Haha... in hindsight I think she did it on purpose, you know."

The Yogi bites his lip apprehensively. "And what about your clothes? Does she have any of your shirts. A black one maybe?"

Luca shakes his head in frustration. "Yeah, probably. I left a lot of my stuff at hers."

"And finally, the shoes. Does she have a pair of your shoes?"

"Yes, YES! When we first broke up, she took some of my clothes and trainers and spray painted "CHEAT" over them."

The Yogi nods again and contemplates for a moment. Luca waits patiently, completely oblivious and uninterested in anything else going on around him.

"Because she has these things, she has the power over you my friend. Because of this your hair is not healthy, you eat and exercise but stay skinny, you are attractive but cannot find love nor happiness. I am right,? I tell you this is why."

Luca looks away shamefully. "I can't believe I thought it was my classmate Mohammed, this whole time."

The Yogi chuckles. "It's normal to be confused and doubtful when you are accursed. But I can assure you, your friend is not to blame here."

"I know." Luca sighs. "I guess I just interpreted his concern as jealously, when in fact he must've been watching out for me."

"No harm, no foul. This is what they say, no?" offers the Yogi, turning his palms up to the sky.

"So... what can I do?" Luca pleads in desperation.

"Don't worry my friend. I will help you..."

The Yogi reaches out and takes both of Luca's hands in his own. They turn and face each other directly; the Yogi closes his eyes and breathes in deeply. Luca in turn, does the same.

The Yogi chants a mantra and systematically clears Luca's aura of negative energy. After running his hand over Luca and shaking away the bad vibes, the Yogi presses his palm against Luca's forehead, right where his third eye ought to be.

"On a Tuesday, you must not cut your hair… or your nails. It is not good to cut these things so much. They have incredibly special powers you see?"

The Yogi pauses again and thinks. Luca sits quietly, eyes still closed. "Every Wednesday, no sex. Sex no good. You must keep this energy for yourself. And on a Thursday, no wear black clothes. OK?"

Luca affirms, yes.

"Good. Now one more thing. Every Saturday…. You buy a loaf of bread; you go outside and break some. Feed to the birds. This is very, very important, yes? This shows appreciation to God. To creation. Don't forget OK!"

They both open their eyes and look at one another. The Yogi smiles reassuringly and lets go of Luca's hands. Luca smiles back and relaxes himself once more, wiping the moisture from his face with his cuff.

"I can't believe it; I feel so much better already." Luca exclaims.

"This is a good sign. Very good. See, I told you. No worries."

"It's like a weight has been lifted off my shoulders!" Luca adds.

"Wait, I have more to say... Your number. You have a special number, correct?"

"Uh, a lucky number? Yeah..."

"Write it down." The Yogi says, handing Luca the back of a receipt and a small, stubby pencil.

Luca obliges and writes down the number '33'. He folds up the receipt and clenches it in between his fist. The Yogi then puts one hand above Luca's fist and the other below. He closes his eyes and mumbles.

"It is 3."

"Close. Well, 33..." corrects Luca.

"No, it is 3. 3 or 1 third is 33.3 continued. But 3 separate parts make the whole. Like the Holy Trinity. Or three siblings. Like you and your sisters."

The usually stubborn and unpersuasive Luca is barley surprised at this point. There seems no use in denying it or even questioning it anymore. Help has come and he dare not miss this opportunity to put things right. "Yes, I have two sisters." Confirms Luca.

"Yes. And all three of you have special gifts. One sister in particular, she is psychic."

"Tatianna?!" Luca states without hesitation.

"You know of which one I speak." assures the Yogi.

"I do." Luca responds calmly.

The park is practically empty now, save for an older lady walking her dog on the opposite side. A rare occurrence in the centre of London, on a busy Monday morning, on a hot summer's day like this.

"Now sir, go and live your life. Be happy, no worries. I will take of these problems for you. As long as you do what I have told you. Soon you will meet a new girl, but you must approach her if you wish to pursue this. In time you will also be given a big opportunity. You must say yes, even if you feel you're not ready."

Luca listens on intently, nodding at the end of every sentence.

"We are brothers now you and me. If you ever need help, you can call on me. Now go, follow your dreams! Teach other people how to live in the right way too. This is your purpose."

"Thank you so much. You don't how much this means to me."

The two stand up from the bench and embrace in a brotherly hug. The Yogi takes out a card with his name and number on it and hands it to Luca. They hug again and shake hands.

Yogi: "You work your job, yes. A good job too, but just for food and money. You must give more than this to the world. But first you must forgive, forget, and love! Good luck dear friend, God loves you."

Luca: "I understand. Thanks again and God bless you too!"

With that, the two men go their separate ways. Luca checks his watch and it is 13:53PM. He has seven minutes to get to his train. Looking back one last time, Luca can just make out the Yogi fading into the bustling London crowds. Luca smiles to himself once more and looks up to the sky. "Thank you." He mutters.

* * *

Later that evening and Luca is back at home in bed, after a wonderful weekend away. Back in the house where he was born; albeit in a different room. In fact he has come full circle really, from a small country town, to the big capital city and all the way back home again.

As he sleeps, he dreams about all he has gained and all he has lost on his journey so far. A bittersweet memory of both accomplishments and lessons learned. Well, hopefully anyway. There is just one thing that is still pressing though. And tonight is the night it must be addressed.

Luca continues to sleep on, cuddling his childhood kangaroo plushy while he does. Outside the once still sky starts to swirl and sway with the wind, as a storm front swiftly rolls in over the sleeping town. Unbeknownst to Luca, the true mastermind or "genius" behind his ongoing torment is about to reveal themself...

Luca's gentle breathing starts to strain and he wheezes again and again, searching for air. Then the temperature suddenly drops and Luca's lips dry and crack, turning a dark blue. Steam comes from his mouth and his body shivers bitterly.

Wrapping the blankets around him, Luca starts to twitch and then shake violently. Simultaneously, the sky outside snaps in a flash of pure white light, followed by the bellowing roar of thunder and the rising pitter-patter of rain.

Luca's eyes open a crack, his vision burry and unclear. He can just about see the outline of the bedroom door and the warm orange glow of the hall light, seeping in through the cracks. Luca strains his eyes and tries to focus. As the image stabilizes, Luca notices a large black shadow come from behind the door and black out the small stream of penetrating light.

Luca lays helpless and paralysed in total darkness, as an invisible force exerts pressure on the door. Luca tries to calm himself but his fear quickly overcomes and consumes him. The colour drains from his skin, his temperature sky rockets; this is it!

The rain now claws at the windows and walls outside

relentlessly, whilst thunder and lightning continue to joust miles above in the heavens.

Luca scans the room again. A first glance reveals nothing amiss but on a second look, Luca notices a thick black smoke begin to filter in from under the door. Luca closes his eyes. All he can see is blackness. He keeps his eyes shut tight, as a shadow begins to form within the thick black smoke at the end of his bed.

Within seconds, the smoke has formed into the shape of a man, around 6 or 7 feet tall. Luca grips his quilt tighter as the atmosphere in the room is leeched of energy and the djinn decides to reveal itself. Luca's eyes peak open.

He sees his assailant at the foot of the bed, stretching its body out in corrupt and contorted ways. The djinn's bones cracking and snapping, as it adjusts to the unfamiliar and material constrictions of the physical plane. The black and grey smoke eventually evaporates away into the air as the djinn becomes "real".

Luca stares on, hypnotized in horror at what he is witnessing. The djinn is stony-grey in colour with electric blue veins marking its rough, dry skin like lightning scars. Imprinted on top of that are tattoos or brands of some kind, that appear to be an ancient Arabic lettering or hieroglyph of some kind.

The creature growls in a low guttural sound and then sniffs the air around him. As it "feels" its way around the room, Luca notices that the djinn is wearing some sort of traditional Middle-Eastern cotton pants.

They're torn and soiled but Luca can just about make out the faded colour and hem lining from the waist down. Adorning its intricate and ornate buckle is a rusted, golden dagger, patterned with special symbols and sigils.

The creature stops abruptly and focuses its attention on Luca's direction. Luca is overwhelmed by the strength of the djinn and its abnormally focused hate towards him. Luca starts to cry. The djinn flexes its sinewy muscles and tastes the air with the tip of its tongue.

Luca opens his mouth to scream but -*WOOSH*, the djinn is already on top of him, wrapping its hands firmly around his neck. Luca squeals. The djinn just growls and grips tighter, causing the chains locked arounds its wrists to clink and clatter against the bedframe.

Luca is finally forced to look the monster straight in the eye and face his demons head on, once and for all. Luca steadies his nerves and opens his eyes slowly and purposefully, staring dead ahead. The djinn looks up and opens its eyelids, revealing crimson red eyes with black reptilian slits in the middle. "He… help…" Luca begs.

The djinn sniffs Luca's aura and opens its abnormally wide mouth to reveal two sets of razor sharp teeth and a long slithery tongue like a snake. Luca realizes something in that instant; he's not dreaming anymore. Or at least it doesn't feel like it, he could swear this is real.

No, this time he is completely conscious, albeit frozen in dread and despite all his best efforts he still can't co-ordinate his actions, form an escape or attack his aggressor. Luca closes his eyes again, unsure of himself. "Ple… please…"

The djinn pauses, it reads Luca's terrified expression in amusement. It tilts its head to either side and analyses its prey's features, taking it all in and savouring every ounce of fear before it devours Luca whole. "Stop it, let me go..." Luca stutters again.

"Haha, foolish lump of clay... you have no say in this matter. I am the one with the power now!"

Luca's shocked, it talks! And in what sounds like a North African accent, with the hint of a snake's hiss when it pronounces its s's.

"What... what do you want from me?" Luca asks.

"You have been found wanting and I am the one who has been tasssked with coming to collect."

"But I've done nothing wrong; I'm a good person."

"WRONG!" the djinn bellows. "You are weak, ssspineless..."

"No, you're wrong."

"Am I? Would you swear your life on it?"

Luca stutters.

The djinn continues: "No, you are full of sssin and sadness, you reek of it!"

Luca's tears are streaming now. He is overwhelmed and exhausted already. He decides to pray. "Oh Dear Lord, whom art in heaven, hallow-"

"Pah!" Scoffs the djinn. "You FOOL!" it yells, shaking Luca violently. Luca presses on, determined.

"Hallowed be your names. Your kingdom come, your wills be done, here on Earth as it is above-"

"Your "God" cares not for your pitiful cries. You have betrayed his honour, you are alone now."

"-give us this day, our daily bread."

The djinn laughs mercilessly. "Haha. You have been abandoned. You should pray to meee."

"No, never!" Luca exclaims.

The djinn runs the tip of its five-inch, pointed nail along Luca's cheek. "You are a wolf in sheep's clothing. You claim to be good and righteous. A man of peace, of purpose. But I know your true ssself…"

"No…" Luca whimpers.

"Yes! And I am the dragon. The serpent in the pit of your stomach. The unbridled fire of your true heart's desire. I was once Ahmed Amir Bin Yeshua. Now I am Amon Baal Zepar; collector of souls!"

"Lies. All lies. You are a liar. You don't exist. This is a dream. I'll wake up any second now."

"Lies? LIES! Then why do you covet that which is not yoursss? Why do you claim to be honest, trustworthy, loyal... when in fact you are not?"

Luca's big brown eyes dart open even wider, and his pupils dilate as he mentally connects the dots. The djinn "Amon Baal Zepar" now "Ahmed-Amir Bin Yeshua" points directly at Luca's heart and jabs it with its needle like nails; one hand still clasped around Luca's throat. The Djinn leans in and sprays spittle all over Luca's face as it snarls:

"On the surface you play one role but underneath; inside, you harbour a desire for lust, laziness and gluttony."

Luca gargles and sputters, trying to speak.

"Not to mention the sssweetest sin of all: Pride!" adds Ahmed in spite, lessening his grip ever so slightly.

Luca coughs and croaks: "No, it's not like that…"

Amon leans in even closer to Luca's face and snaps his serrated teeth centimeteres from Luca's nose: "Argh!"

Luca winces, truly terrified.

"You really don't recall, do you?

Amon chuckles devilishly to himself, before raising his free arm and fully extending his clawed hand like a set of kitchen knives -SHING!

"You once prayed to me, as a young man… you said: "I would give anything, nay EVERYTHING, just to be admired and lusted after" like my friends!"

Luca looks on in horror. He closes his eyes and thinks back to everything that has happened. How he got to this very moment and why.

"I fulfilled your wishhh, and now you must fulfill mine."

Luca sheds a single tear, that seems to roll in slow-motion over his cheek, down his chin and drop onto the floor. In that split second, he has an epiphany. This creature, this djinn; Amon or Ahmed, whatever! He feeds off Lucas fear; his shame, his guilt.

But all creatures are created equal and imperfect, our dark sides need to be embraced to be overcome. Not just fought off or continually feared. Otherwise they only come back, again and again, faster and stronger. Luca finally speaks: "I... I..."

Amon: "What now, petulant man-child!"

"I'm a coward! OK, is that what you want to hear?" Luca screams in defiance.

Amon tilts his head curiously and smiles menacingly, intrigued. "Hm, go on..."

"The relationship was toxic from the start. We fought for control constantly, and never admitted our true feelings or desires. She's not to blame, I am. I didn't have the courage or the heart to do the right thing and end it. I was afraid!"

Ahmed lowers his attacking arm slightly: "Ah, the sssins of the Father have finally come home; yesss, you truly are your Grandfather's heir. The apple falls not far from the tree... Womanizers and Casanovas to the last. You know your Grandfather once prayed to me too!"

Luca continues: "Yes, I was afraid. Afraid of her reaction, afraid of hurting her, afraid of the shame, the guilt, the failure!"

Amon smirks, his eyes flash a brighter, bloodier, piercing red.

"Karma is an echo that ripples throughout time. Now you must pay for both his sinsss and yoursss!"

With that, Amon places both hands on either side of Luca's head, practically covering his entire face. Then he pulls Luca in closer and opens wide his impossibly jointed jaw. As his nails dig deeper into Luca's skin, on the side of his face, it forces Luca to scream out in pain. Amon seizes the opportunity and lines up their mouths, attempting to possess Luca's soul.

Mouth forced open wide, the djinn's "essence" or "spirit" begins to leave Ahmed and drive its way inside Luca.

As the energy levels increase in the room, everything vibrates and a high pitched frequency begins to ring. Luca's eyes glaze over white as he loses his battle for control over his physical body. While the energy continues to intensify, darts of electricity zap and crackle, shooting sparks of blue lights in all directions.

Luca starts to hallucinate. He sees the day he was born; his mother, his father, his grandparents. He sees Nonno Pietro holding him as a child and whispering "Buon fortuna "Faccia Lisce"…" (Good luck, "Smooth Face"…).

Then he sees himself growing up, the good times and the bad. Holidays, school, games, arguments, bullying, fighting. He sees his first kiss, his first heartbreak, he sees Arabella and their entire relationship. From there, everything speeds up progressively and fast-forwards right up to this present moment.

Snapping back to the here and now, Luca has another revelation; an epiphany. The mistakes he has made in the past don't define him. What defines him is who he is as a person, what he stands for and what he believes in. That is the sentiment that matters the most. And now Luca suddenly knows what he has to do.

"You'll never do it. You're too weak!" the djinn mocks. "I am an Ifrit! The most powerful of Djinn. Your resistance only prolongs your deathhh."

Luca whispers to himself: "Lord lead me away from all temptation, deliver me from the evil you have created. Forgive me for my sins; past, present, and future. Allow me to make things right."

With those words Luca's left hand suddenly comes alive, it flinches fractionally at first, then again and again, until it's finally loose. This ignites a chain reaction which soon spreads across his whole being, bringing him back to life.

His astral body and physical body merge back together and become one again, fighting off the invading djinn's spirit. Luca, realizing that his faith and belief is what is helping him, relaxes his mind, body, and spirit.

"You are only a projection of my deepest, darkest fears and desires. Brought about by untamed love and passion.

Manipulated by entities like you…callous, blasphemous, envious creatures, whose only purpose is to turn good people away from God. You listen to *me* now. You have no more power here!"

The djinn spirit is pushed back up and out of Luca. Amon, upon realizing what is happening, lets out a blood curdling screech and frantically tries to regain control. "Argh, NO! You can't possibly overcome meee, it's impossible. Your sssoul was mine, I owned you!"

Luca musters all the strength and courage he can. Luca: "Nothing is impossible, just ask God."

Amon looks surprisingly afraid for the first time and loosens his grip from Luca slightly. Upon noticing this, Luca is filled with a sudden surge of confidence and firms his stance accordingly. Amon's arms go weak in response and his grip lessens even further.

"In the name of all that is Holy and good, be gone Djinn! I cast you OUT!"

That is when the forces of light and love overcome the

darkness and hate, and Luca is instantly reenergised with all the strength he needs. He explodes into action, his pupils returning to his eyes and his body bursting to life. Luca throws his fists at Amon instinctively. Nothing seems to connect at first and there is a barbaric thrashing of legs, hands, and teeth.

Eventually Amon is beaten back into the centre of the room and Luca quickly seizes the opportunity, continuing to pummel the creature relentlessly. From the spirit realm, all of Luca's ancestors, spirit guides, guardian angels and soul mates appear. They cross the veil and give their power and energy in support of Luca's fight.

The more Luca attacks, the smaller and weaker the djinn gets. Reverting from its tall, grotesque form into something that resembles more of a man. A man who was once called Ahmed; the person it used to be.

Luca pauses. He looks down at this broken, beaten, and bitter shell of a man in his true form, for the first time. He takes a moment to pity the hatred that his opponent must harbour in his heart and shakes his head in resentment. Ahmed looks up at Luca, quivering in embarrassment.

"You should know, there are worse things out there than me boy..." Luca looks back to his spirit guides, who are glowing a magnificent multitude of colours. They smile and nod reassuringly, glowing brighter to show their support.

Luca turns back around and takes one last look at Ahmed, whose currently curled up like a fetus in the middle of the bedroom floor. Luca takes some time to catch his breath. He clutches his neck and rubs it gently; there are visible bruises left from the djinn's attack. From there he runs his hand down his chest, and clutches Chiara's blue opal necklace. Grasping it tighter, he whispers a small, personal prayer and makes the sign of the cross.

Ahmed reaches out shakily with one impious hand. "You think you have the power now? Your power is but an illusion, like this physical world you covet so much. Iblis is the only one with power here, Iblis and his Archons. You are all mere pretenders to the throne, locked in a cage." .

Luca steadies himself, brings his hands together in prayer and breaths in deeply. He looks Ahmed directly in the eyes and speaks in a firm and unflinching tone: "If this place is a prison, then why do you want in so much?"

As he breathes out, a magnificent white blinding-light exudes from all his pores, casting a blanket of holy fire over everything within sight. Luca drops to the bedroom floor as the light fades back into his pores and the room falls into darkness once again. He kneels alone at the end of his bed, the room a complete mess. Books are littered all over the place, the curtains have fallen down and pillow feathers are floating through the air.

He looks around and contemplates both the wreck around him, and the night's incredible events. He smiles to himself. He knows he has finally passed the test. Now he can actually move on. Now he can live life again. Luca closes his eyes and submits to sleep, completely worn out by his torturous tussle with the djinni. He falls into a deep, peaceful sleep and awakens hours later, to find himself tucked up back in his bed.

He looks around and is bewildered to find that his room is completely untouched. There are no books on the floor, no broken curtain rails and no fluff from gutted pillows. Luca rubs his eyes thoroughly, to make sure he's not in fact still dreaming but it still just as surprised to find everything fixed and orderly.

Luca mouths "What the fuck." to himself and picks his watch up off the dresser, checking the time. It's almost 1:00PM in the afternoon! Scratching his head, Luca falls back into bed and throws his watch down on the quilt.

He runs his hands through his hair as he adjusts to his new reality, one finally without the threat of psychological or spiritual attack. Pulling the quilts up again, Luca snuggles back to sleep and decides to savour the moment. It's not like he's slept well in years and besides, after last night, he feels he's earnt it.

Closing his eyes tight once more, Luca nods off in comfort, because even if he has no physical evidence from his confrontation… the weight that has been lifted off his shoulders is proof enough for him.

"The fact that if one tries beyond one's capacity to be perfect, the shadow descends into hell and becomes the devil."

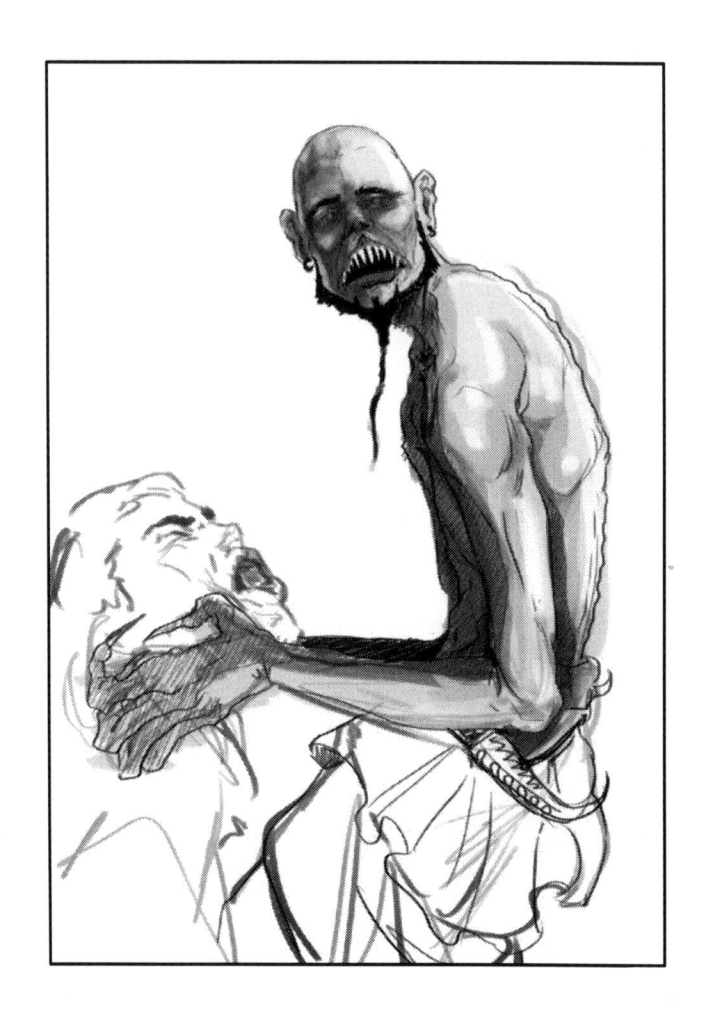

ACCURSED

Chapter 8

Accursed

Months have now passed since Luca's last visit by the djinn. He sits quietly, alone, back where he started, in Bristol at his family home. Today he is perched in front of an old desktop computer, in the corner of his parents dining room; the song *"La Ritournelle by Sebastian Tellier"* playing on in the background.

A word document is akready open and ready on the screen but Luca is preoccupied, looking out through the large patio windows to his left.

The summer sun shimmers like crystals on the garden pond and the grass glows a gorgeous jasmine shade of green. Off to one side, Luca's vegetable patch already has a healthy growth of olives, figs and strawberries. While on the other, his newly planted grape vine sprawls over the slabbed patio, creating a natural canopy of sorts.

Luca looks back to his work. He nods to himself for reassurance, clicks his knuckles and then starts to type…

"The Curse of Faccia Lisce: My Djinn Diaries

by Luca Vincenzo DiMarco.

Part III - Conclusions: So that sums up my story so far, although I do realise it's still far from the end. Take what you have read and interpret it how you will. I am not trying to convince anyone of anything or make them believers in something that they're not. However if even one person is encouraged to take on their own spiritual journey after reading this, then I will consider my job done.

Having said that, the real message of this bitter-sweet tale is forgiveness. Forgiveness for your enemies. Forgiveness for your friends. And most importantly, forgiveness for yourself. Learn from your mistakes and miss-steps and find strength in your faults. For one cannot be truly wise, without first failing."

Luca pauses from typing and takes a sip of green tea from his mug, which is labelled with the encouragingly humorous phrase: "Keep Calm & Carry Crystals". For the first time in a long time, Luca is truly living in the present moment and that means really savouring each taste. He ponders for a second and takes another sip, smiling as three magpies land on the lawn just outside the window. Luca one again inhales the soothing scents of his herbal drink, before going back to work.

"An update on my situation: I'm still doing everything the Yogi told me to do. I don't cut my hair on Tuesdays, and when I do cut it, it's only a light trim. (I have been reading about how hair is like an antenna and holds information, connecting us to our roots: mother nature). In fact, I am growing my beard out now too and embracing my curls again. My sex life is active, although not frequent in the slightest. More so, if and when I do engage; I certainly avoid Wednesdays (haha) and it's only with someone I truly care about or have a genuine connection with.

Admittedly I do wear black sometimes, but that is mostly just because of work. Besides, the main thing is that the night terrors have stopped completely now. In fact, within the first two weeks of undertaking these tasks, the djinn steadily appeared less and less. Until ultimately, they eventually just vanished all together!"

Luca stops again for a moment. He reads back what he just wrote to himself and scratches his bread. This means a lot to him. This is his catharsis. Luca mutters to himself as he tries to verbalise his thoughts, and then pushes on.

"Now? Now I just live every day, one day at a time. And if things don't go my way the first time around, I tell myself it's probably a lesson. I.E: what can it teach me? And when that lesson does come around, no matter how long it takes, I see it as a blessing and not a curse. Besides, "better late than never" right? It's a saying that has served me well recently and hasn't let me down so far.

So on top of all this, I try my best to avoid things that may be bad for me. Things like smoking or drinking, etc. But if I really have to do it, then I do it in strict moderation. A _balanced_ life is the key, for we will never fully get rid of our darker parts or our shadow-selves. We can only learn to live with them and through them, *without* allowing them to control us. I know what you're thinking: "Easier said than done". But believe me, it is achievable; with hard work and perseverance! No it will not be easy, and no, it was never meant to be. And any perceived "success" will not last forever either. This is something that we have to continually work on, throughout our many, many lifetimes...

I did find a new job though; you'll be glad to hear. It's probably temporary but it's one that pays well and treats me a lot better as an employee. I haven't' found love, yet but I'm OK with that. And despite appearances, I am over "her" and that for me, is enough right now. One step at a time. Slow and steady wins the race.

"Piano, piano." (Slowly, slowly). What happens next? I have no clue. Haha! But I do know that I am ready for it, whatever it is, whenever it decides to come... The End."

With that, Luca saves the file one last time and switches off the computer. He gets up slowly and purposefully, totally in the present moment, and heads outside and onto the grass, barefoot. Eventually Luca makes it to middle of the garden and digs his feet gently and deeply into the cool, damp Earth.

He looks up to the big, beautiful, baby-blue sky and lets the sun shine on down. Allowing the light to penetrate right through him, as he quietly and confidently meditates with his mind.

As Luca enters into a deeper state of tranquility, he imagines a rainbow coloured aura surrounding his body. It radiates a gorgeous golden light that includes all the hues of the spectrum. As this glow grows and illuminates all the hidden spaces of the back garden, it also drives out any previously unseen spirits from their hiding places.

That's right, the faint vibrational screams of djinn being expelled from the vicinity echo through the air. Luca is unafraid however and can only smile and let the love surround him. Whilst he slips deeper into tranquility and awareness, he imagines a third eye made of light, opening up in the centre of his forehead. Allowing this newfound ability time to adjust and focus, Luca slowly lowers himself into the lotus position on the grass and breathes in fully.

As Luca's mind awakens fully to the extent of this illusory matrix, so too does his heart open up to the truth that everything is unconditional love. Then, from out of Luca's aura steps another being made of light, a being that approximates the shape and size of Luca himself. That's because it is, in fact, Luca himself, or at least his "higher-self".

Luca pauses, acknowledging this "best version" of him and likewise it too does the same back. Then telepathically it asks Luca: "Hello dear friend, where would you like to go today?" Luca grins; as well as no longer being afraid, he is also no longer unsure. Instead, he centres his "chi-energy" and astral projects out of his body. Then, whilst focusing on a particular location with his mind, levitates off the ground.

The two doppelgangers rise higher and higher off the ground, before being whisked up into the air and above the city streets. Climbing higher, further, faster, they look down at the hustle and bustle of the city streets below. Luca can see a multitude of people going about their business; some enlightened and others not so. Some already damned by their own demons, and others guided by beguiling guardian angels.

Eventually they both reach the upper-outer atmosphere and shoot out into space, piercing the plethora. Pushing past the planets and riding on straight through the endless sea of starry souls.

Luca and his spirit guide continue to speed up, until they are travelling at the speed of light and ultimately explode into the heart of the universe, revealing its true nature. A large, swirling vortex of energy and consciousness, that simply resembles an eye. An all seeing eye. God's eye.

"Your experiences do not form you; you form yourself by understanding your experiences."

Epilogue

Arabella is now also back in her home town, sat cross-legged and statuesque on her bed, which lies tucked into the corner of her cramped but cozy bedroom. Scattered atop her dresser are an exotic variety of flickering, scented candles and incense sticks. The smoke they gradually release, gently dances and swirls in the air, forming a hazy mist around the room.

Now and again, Arabella sways slightly on the spot, as she mumbles some inaudible words to herself. The words form a sort of chant, Arabic or Middle Eastern sounding in nature. After reaching a quiet crescendo, she lets out a long, drawn-out sigh and drops to her mattress.

Momentarily regaining her breath, Arabella slowly lifts up her head and confidently blows out all the candles on the side. She watches on as the puffs of smoke bellow up into the air and congregate in the ceiling corners.

As they stretch and strain above her head, the smoke temporarily appears to take the form of a djinn, before trailing off again into invisible atoms. Reforming her lotus position on the bed, Arabella looks back down and opens her palm.

In the centre of her hand lies her father's old signet ring, the very same one she revealed to Luca back in London at university. The very same one that Khalid found all those years ago, in a stream in Amezrou, Morocco. The very same one that trapped a genie; a demon, named Amon Baal Zepar all those millennia ago.

If one were to look closely at the ring, they would see that the emblem is almost alive with a crimson red highlight that runs all the way through the engravings. Look even closer into the solid, black opal-gem, and there a shadow lurks in the inky-black void. A shadow with form and shape, with mind and motive, with hopes and desires.

A shadow bound to this inanimate object, cursed for all eternity to tip-toe the line between worlds, but never truly be a part of either. A shadow we now know as the Djinn! A race of creatures created by God, just like man, who long to be a part of this physical world once more. Instead they are bound to inhabit the astral plane, stuck between heaven and earth forever more.

Arabella frowns as she contemplates on all that has transpired. Her frown fades as she breathes in deeper, intentionally calming her mind and emotions. Eventually Arabella's anger is replaced by indifference, and after a few more moments; apathy. Contented, she throws the ring up it the air and catches it with her other hand. Popping it nonchalantly into her pocket, she hops off her bed and leaves the room, locking the door behind her.

Left out in the middle of her bed, is a photograph of Luca, a couple of his personal possessions and a lock of his hair. Now downstairs and socializing with her family, Arabella finally sounds genuinely happy. Marking the beginning of her own spiritual journey to move on. Balance would seem to have been restored, for now. Or has it?

Back in Arabella's room, a spindly, dark-blue, feminine hand (with especially long, raggedy nails and an assortment of tribal beads around her wrists), reaches out from the shadows and snatches Luca's picture. The unknown intruder snarls:

"He belongsss to meee... goddesss of the deep...."

And then dissipates back into the darkness, leaving a trail of saltwater and seaweed in its wake.

The End.

"Your cells are constantly renewed. You always have another chance to recreate yourself."

Afterword

Although not a biographical account, this story was inspired, in part, on real events that took place circa 2011. This book was written with the simple aim to enlighten people. Especially those who might not know otherwise, about the djinn and their role in our histories, cultures, religions and mythologies (whether they are indeed real or not).

It is also hoped that this book will encourage other people, who have also experienced sinister, supernatural, or surreal events in their lives; to research deeper into esoteric knowledge themselves. You may just find some of the answers you are looking for…

Above all else, "*Accursed: The Djinn Chronicles*" is meant to entertain, so please do not be frightened or anxious about any of the themes raised here. The simple truth is: everything comes from love, and back to love is where everything will return. So fear not the unknown or that which you believe to be evil or ugly, because everything has its place and was designed with a purpose.

Moreover, you are protected by your spirit guides, ancient ancestors, higher-selves, guardian angels and more… you just have to ask for help!

Some good books to read as further research into the djinn, symbols, religion, and ancient history, are listed at the end of this book. Thank you all for reading, I really hope it has connected with you in some way. Until next time: stay safe, stay well, stay blessed, namaste.

"Don't talk, act. Don't say, show. Don't promise, prove."

Terminology

DJINN CLASSES:

"Shayatin" (Arabic: شياطين, shayāṭīn) – Meaning "devils" or "demons", are generic evil spirits in Islamic belief, instructing humans to sin by whispering in their hearts. In essence, it is their nature to lead humans astray or behave mischievously. Furthermore the word "shayatin" literally means "distant" or "astray", connotating that these creatures are distant from divine mercy. They are by far the most common type of djinn.

"Ghul" (Arabic: غول, ghūl) – A Ghul or "Ghoul", is another demon-like being or monstrous humanoid, originating in pre-Islamic Arabian religion. Normally they are associated with

graveyards and the consumption of human flesh. Some even state that Ghul's are desert dwelling, shape-shifting demons that can assume the guise of animals.

"Ifrit" (Arabic: عفريت, ifrīt) - Also spelt "Efreet" or "Afrit", are a powerful class of demon in Islamic mythology. They are heavily associated with the underworld and are also thought to represent the spirits of the dead. According to traditional folklore, the Ifrit are said to inhabit desolate places such as ruins or temples. They are extremely powerful and usually malevolent. Both "genies" (djinni or djinn) featured in the animated movie *"Aladdin"* (1992) are in fact Ifrits. Furthermore, the blue colouring of Robin William's character and the red markings of "Jafar", signify the djinns ability to be both benevolent and malevolent in nature.

"Marid" (Arabic: مارد mārid) – Marids are often seen as the most formidable type of djinn in Arabic, pre-Islamic and Islamic folklore. The root word for "marid" means "rebel" or "rebellious". They are also associated with the elements and are

believed to move both on the wind or with the sea. They also have the ability to summon and control extreme weather at their own will. In western culture, they are sometimes confused with "mermaids", "sirens" or "banshees". In African mythologies they are recognised as "apeths", as seen in the 2020 Netflix thriller film *"His House"*.

SYMBOLS & SIGILS:

"Seal of Solomon" (Arabic: خاتم سليمان Khātam Sulaymān) – Also known as the "Ring of Solomon", is a six-pointed star or hexagram that is commonly used as an invocation symbol, to both summon and ensnare wandering spirits or demons (djinn). In one infamous Biblical story, King Solomon is gifted the signet ring from God, as a means to control djinn. This power was bestowed upon him not only because he was a wise and just ruler, but because when offered anything by God, Solomon asked only for more knowledge and wisdom to better help his people.

"Eye of Ra" (also called a "wadjet" or "wedjat") – The right "Eye of Ra" or "Eye or Re" (not to be confused with the left "Eye of Horus"), is a protective symbol that represents the sun, royal power and good health. It also functions as a feminine counterpart to the Egyptian sun god Ra and represents the aggressive, passionate and protective force that subdues his enemies.

"Hand of Fatima" (aka the "Hamsa Hand") – Is an ancient Middle-Eastern amulet that symbolises the hand of God. It also represents femininity and the feminine aspect of God. It is often referred to as "the woman's holy hand". It brings good luck and defends against the "Evil Eye", as well as inciting happiness, good health & material fortune.

OBJECTS OF IMPORTANCE:

"Djinn Ring" – As previously mentioned in the story of King Solomon, it is possible to bind wandering spirits or demons (djinn) with inanimate objects or vessels. This allows the captive entity to be summoned again later at the owners (magicians) will.

"Djinni Lamp" – Much like in the 1940 film *"The Thief of Baghdad"*, or more recently in the Netflix series *"The Witcher"*, djinn are also associated with being imprisoned inside objects. Such items can include but are not limited to; lamps, bottles, vases, chests and gem-stones of various kinds. The genie in the lamp from *"Aladdin"* (2019) is probably the most well-known interpretation of a djinn in Western culture, even birthing the anglicized term "genie". These benevolent, happy and carefree interpretations of djinn are often highly inaccurate, however. Although, that is not to say there aren't good djinn in existence as well.

"Iblis Orb" – ("Iblis" meaning "the Devil" in Arabic). A pendant, necklace or chained orb are often required for trapping and containing the most powerful of djinn. The unique feature of a necklace as opposed to a lamp or bottle; is it allows the owner to keep the "familiar" (returning spirit) on their person at all times. The chain also acts as a second source of "binding", reducing the chance of the entity being able to break free.

TERMS OF INTEREST:

"Sleep Paralysis" – Sleep Paralysis is a sleeping condition that refers to the inability to move or speak, as you are in the process of waking up or falling asleep. Our brains paralyse our bodies when we sleep, to avoid our muscles "acting out" during our dreams. Some sufferers also report seeing and hearing things in the room with them, as they are paralysed.

"Astral Plane" – The astral plane is where our "astral bodies" go when we are sleeping. This is the dimension in which we experience our dreams. It is very similar to our own, only much more fluid and changeable. We call this plane or "realm" the "4th dimension".

"Third Eye" – The "3rd Eye" or "pineal gland" is a small pea-shaped gland in the middle of our brain. It produces melatonin and DMT; the chemicals which control our sleep cycles and dream rhythms. Some believe it is also the source of our "sixth sense" (spiritual intuition) and can be used for telepathy, clairvoyancy, divination and more.

"Al-Kuhl" – The word alcohol is said to have come from the Arabic term "Al-Kuhl" and "Al-Gawl", which means "body eating spirit". This could be why some alcoholic drinks are called "spirits" and "boo-ze". It is also commonly known, in more spiritual parts of the world, that drinking alcohol is one of the fastest ways to lower your soul's vibration. In fact, many theologists and philosophers agree that alcohol has been used by governments and institutions, to keep human consciousness at a lowered state for thousands of years.

"Iblis (The Devil) himself recognizes the Lordship of Allah (God), but he wants human beings to forget it."

ACCURSED

References

BOOKS:

- *"The Djinn Connection"* by Rosemary Ellen Guiley
- *"Legend of the Fire Spirits"* by Robert Lebling
- *"Serpent of Wisdom"* by Donald Tyson
- *"As Above, So Below"* by Alan Oken
- *"The Hermetica"* by Timothy Freke & Peter Gandy
- *"The Symbol Detective"* by Tony Allan
- *"Short Introduction To Religion"* by Gordon Kerr
- *"Awake"* by Tobias Hamilton
- *"Stepping into the Magic"* by Jill Edwards
- *"The Alchemist"* by Paulo Coelho
- *"The Gift of the Jews"* by Thomas Cahill

FILMS:

- *"Under the Shadow"* (2016)
- *"Underworld: Legend of the Jinn"* (2014)
- *"Djinn"* (2013)
- *"The Shadow People"* (2012)
- *"Stranded" / "Djinns"* (2010)
- *"Red Sands"* (2009)
- *"Long Time Dead"* (2002)
- *"Wishmaster"* (1997)
- *"Aladdin"* (1992)
- *"The Outing"* (1987)
- The Thief of Bagdad (1940)

"We are all connected. To each other, biologically. To the earth, chemically. To the rest of the universe atomically."

ACCURSED

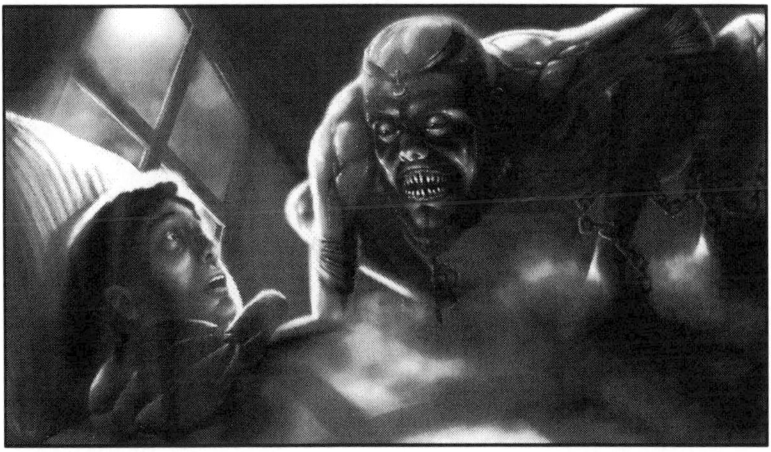

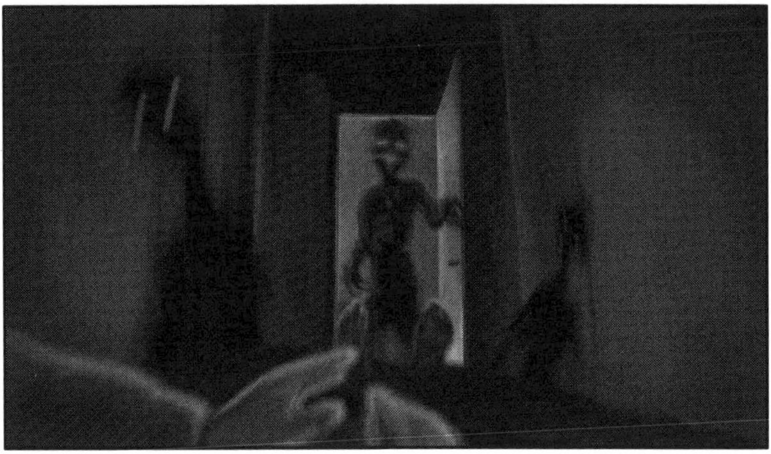

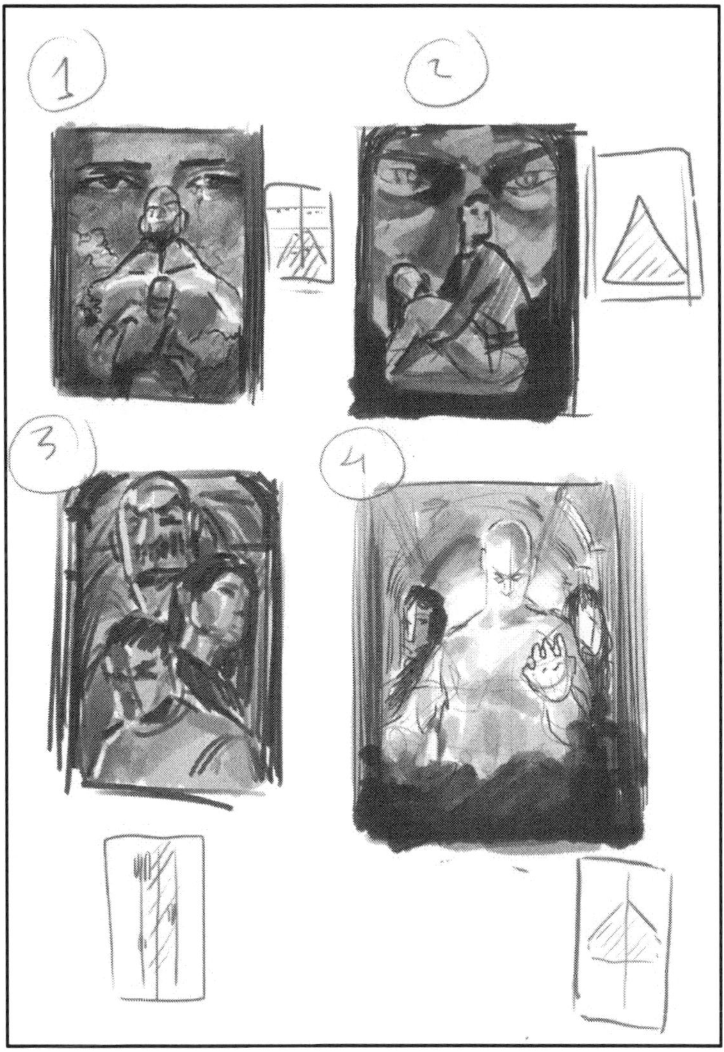
1
2
3
4

"Mektoub" (It is written)

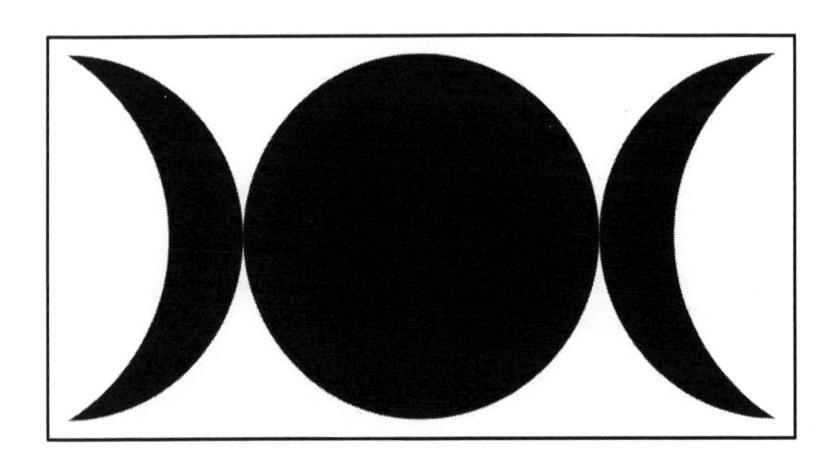

FIN

Printed in Great Britain
by Amazon